# Elizabeth Arnold

Elizabeth Arnold was born in Leicester but has moved about quite a bit during childhood and adulthood. She is married with two adult children and now lives in Southampton. Elizabeth has always enjoyed writing and used her talents in many different forms like diaries, reports and articles before she wrote her first novel, *The Parsley Parcel*.

Her love of exploring and her inquisitive nature have helped her immensely in her work, especially in preparation for the *Freya* trilogy, which required her to do research into the Romany culture. Many of her ideas and much of her writing are inspired by her interest in nature, the elements and a desire to know about lifestyles and cultures which display a sense of freedom.

**Also by Elizabeth Arnold**

The Freya Trilogy:

The Parsley Parcel
*Shortlisted for the Beefeater Children's Novel
Award*

Gold and Silver Water
*Commended for the TES/NASEN Special
Educational Needs Award*

A Riot of Red Ribbon


**Mammoth Storybooks for young readers:**

Scraggy Flies High
Thief in the Garden

# Contents

# Spin Elizabeth Arnold of the Sunwheel

mammoth

For my much loved daughters
Lizan Jane and Kerri Anne

First published in Great Britain in 1999 by Mammoth
an imprint of Egmont Children's Books Limited
Michelin House, 81 Fulham Road, London SW3 6RB

ISBN 0 7497 3389 6

10 9 8 7 6 5 4 3 2 1

A CIP catalogue record for this book
is available from the British Library

Typeset by Avon Dataset Ltd, Bidford on Avon, B50 4JH
Printed in Great Britain by Cox & Wyman Ltd, Reading, Berkshire

# CONTENTS

At first Brigid felt no lightness in her soul. She clung to the limbs that were shaking her into wakefulness, all but dragging them down with her. She rose wearily from the depths of the river, and as she rose her limbs turned to silver, a silver as brittle as her painted-on smile.

It seemed that since time began she had searched the endless rivers. She had walked the centuries until her feet were shredded from the effort, until her heart had been so heavy with hopelessness that Nodens had called her back to rest in the black watery depths of oblivion to sleep, so she might find the strength to rise and start her endless search again.

# 1 Gwen

'You have to come!' Mum screamed.

'I'm not registered!' I reminded them. 'It was you that forgot. I've never been to school either. You leave me here. I'm safer, you're safer. Do you really want to be chased by the social? Nobody cares if I'm not registered here.'

'You can't stay! Not all alone.'

I ignored her. I stalked out of the tiny cabin, Den close at heel, and climbed on to *Brigantia*'s cabin roof. It's my special place. Here I am always left alone.

*Brigantia* is a brightly painted narrow-boat and I feel she is mine. I was born on her and, if I have my way, I will die on her. My heart is fused into her timbers. I am one of the new generation of boat people, and very, very proud of it. For years the canals were not worked, except for bits and bobs in the tourist trade, and *Brigantia* lay neglected. Now industries are beginning to choose water once more for transportation

1

because the roads are so congested. Every day the river and cut become busier. This is my place, my home. I will not leave!

Mum and Dad think I'm strange not bothering to make friends. They worry, saying I wear loneliness wrapped round me like a well-worn blanket. Well, if they're right, it's only a comfort blanket, part of me. I just don't like strangers. I don't need strangers. The dog, Den, and the boat, *Brigantia*, are friends enough for me. You can keep your discos *and* your telly. I can read, I can write, I can think, I can feel. What more do I need?

I feel now as I always have, as if I'm waiting for something special to happen, something to do with river or cut. I just don't know when, or how. Sometimes, when I sit on the cabin roof in the evening, I hear the wind in the leaves calling me, or perhaps it's the quiet movements of the water that endlessly echoes my name. Mum and Dad don't understand, but they weren't born to the boats, not like me.

*Brigantia* is bright and cheerful but there's not much space on-board when the boat and the butty are stuffed to the gunwale with goodies to be dispensed along endless miles of waterways. I don't need a posh house or a huge garden. I have the River Thames. We work the pubs and shops from Windsor to Oxford, and that is playground enough for me.

I know Mum and Dad are worried sick. Grandad is slowly dying. He's very old and can no longer manage alone. The land is calling them back, Grandad is calling them back.

Reluctantly I left my refuge and returned to the fray. 'Leave me here,' I pleaded. 'Someone has to care for *Brigantia*.'

'She can't stay!' my mother said, but the look she gave my father asked, Can she?

'She won't be on her own,' Dad said, pointing to our scruffy, black and white collie.

'No, Den's with me,' I agreed, wondering why the mere mention of his name was sending shivers down my spine.

They argued among themselves for a while. I left them to it. There were locks to be opened, a lay-by to reach before dusk. By the time I returned to the cabin, it was settled. Grandad needed them more than I did.

'You won't be frightened all by yourself?' my mother asked anxiously.

'No, Den's here to take care of me,' I repeated firmly but, despite the brightness of my voice, I felt strangely shivery.

'You'll need a crew,' Dad said.

'I'll find one,' I promised, 'and until I do, I'll manage. You mustn't worry, after all, I'll soon be sixteen. I'm tall and strong and born to this life.'

# 2 Albion

Albion marched across the page. As I read I saw his vast body towering over the nervous villagers who were rushing out of his way. Where the land was soft, his footsteps sank deep and then the villagers smiled, for here, when the rains came, they would have ponds and water aplenty. Trees shook and trembled, falling like matches where Albion and his army brushed them carelessly aside in their haste to reach Gaul . . .

'Gwen!'

I thought for a moment I heard my mother, but she was gone, I heard only the night wind in the canopy trees. I turned back to my book. Albion marched steadily on. I forgot I was hungry. I was there, hiding with the villagers, watching the giants pass, mile after mile, village after village.

'Long live the King!' called an old man, hoping the giant would turn his way and give his village a pond too. 'Long live the King of all Albion!'

His grovelling was wasted. Albion was too busy to stop. He reached the Straits of Dover and stomped angrily across the narrow isthmus, which in those days joined England to France. He didn't want to help his greedy, cattle-rustling brothers, he was a peaceful man; but he was also a man of honour and he had been summoned.

The small army of giants was big and heavy, the isthmus was weak and narrow, the earth trembled and crumbled as they passed. I held my breath, quite sure they would sink into the sea.

When Albion arrived he discovered his brothers fighting Hercules for possession of the red oxen belonging to Geryon. Hercules was catching massive stones from the heavens and hurling them frantically at the heads of the giants who, one by one, stumbled and fell.

Albion fought bravely but it was useless. He saw his brothers die before fleeing back across the isthmus. As he fled to safety, the earth behind him crumbled into the sea. The water, angry at such a disturbance, bubbled up and over, sending huge plumes of steamy froth into the air. Albion barely noticed. He was angry and he was tired. His army and his brothers had all perished, and for what? Albion stamped harder, the furious muddy plumes sprayed high as mountains, the sea boiled and tumbled where once there had been land. The narrow isthmus disappeared for ever.

Albion glanced behind him and felt only relief. Albion

had become an island, England. He and his people would be safe. I wanted him safe! He was big and he was gentle and the villagers loved him.

Only, Albion wasn't safe. A picture showed Brut and Corineus and their huge army crossing an angry sea. The small boats approaching Plymouth Hoe tossed endlessly up and down like spent confetti. A great sea god rose from the waters and commanded the sea to drown the invading hordes, but the army was widely spread. The sea tried hard to obey, but in the foamy chaos many boats reached the English shores. There was much death, and for what purpose?

Once again Albion fought, but I knew now that although giants had great strength, they were not military minded and had little fighting brain. The invading hordes had tempered blades on long poles which were thrust into the arteries of the lumbering giants. Twisted spears entered their bodies, ripping their bellies to pieces as they were withdrawn. Long, light lances, normally used to pierce the heart of a man, were thrust into the eyes and brains of the fallen giants.

The giants didn't stand a chance. They possessed only wooden clubs, no more than hunks of trees gathered in haste on their way to battle. They moved them slowly, far too slowly. It was pathetic to watch. Even so, the battle was very long and very bloody. The giants reached and slashed and stamped as their life blood gushed into the soil. It was so unfair. I cried as one after one they died. When Albion fell, the few remaining giants fled to Cornwall. The battle was over.

The invading armies whooped and shouted with joy. King Brut raised his banner; Corineus stood proudly at his side. The villagers peeped out from their hiding places, trembling in fear. Albion, king and country, were gone for ever.

I couldn't understand why I was so upset. It was a story, a long ago story, but it felt like it was now, it felt like it was part of me.

# 3  The

# accident

The river's mood was eerie. It was the thirty-first of October, the eve of All Souls' Day, Hallowe'en. I was not into pumpkins and witches, but somehow I felt wary, expectant. I had felt uneasy all day and yet everything had gone well. A quarter of my load was sold before I reached the outskirts of London. I leaned on the tiller, weary from lifting and carrying, and waved at old George Cutler as his scruffy old barge passed by on its way back down to the docks.

'Missing your mum and dad, Gwen? Want Johnny to crew a while?'

I grinned. The cut was amazing. There were all these boats, too busy to do more than pause as they passed, and yet everyone knew everything within moments. It was like we were all family.

'No, thanks, George, I pick up my own crew soon.'

George smiled back. I knew he felt relieved. He was becoming very arthritic and really should have stayed retired, but he had returned to catch the new trade and give work to his sons. I blew him a kiss. He's a funny old stick but he's kind. I smiled as I twisted my head round to watch the old man chug on. I hadn't lied to make life easy for him, or out of false pride. I don't know why I lied, I just knew I had to.

'Are you sure?' George checked, blowing me a kiss back.

'Course I'm sure, thanks very much, George. It's a bit more lonely than I expected without Mum worrying about me and Dad nagging me to do something, but I'm fine. I'm happy and managing really well, honest I am.'

'You'll not be so lonely when you get your new crew,' George shouted as his boat and mine drew further apart.

'No,' I yelled back to please him, 'things will be much better then.'

Before long I made my last stop of the day. I smiled fixedly at the gongoozlers, our name for tourists, who sat idly drinking beer as they watched me haul boxes across the towpath and up to the tiny house that served as both pub and shop. I used to ignore them as much as I could but my dad would have none of it. 'They're our customers, Gwen. Smile sweetly and they'll ask questions, buy something extra.' He was right, they usually did.

Jack, the landlord, rustled a couple of helpers up. 'She's on her own, lads. Her grandad's sick . . .' I smiled even more sweetly; sometimes, just sometimes, it helps to be a girl.

One more lock and I could hold-in for the night. Dusk was falling and my muscles ached, but I was satisfied with a day's work well done. I wrote a postcard telling Mum and Dad they should be proud of all my efforts. I hopped off *Brigantia* without cutting the engine and raced along the towpath and up the small slope that edged the bridge to post my card. I scurried breathlessly down the other side and hopped back aboard *Brigantia*, which was emerging from the bridge hole just as I had expected. I looked forward to dipping into the stew that had been quietly simmering on my small stove for hours.

The lock was open as it should be. I cut my engines as I eased *Brigantia* gently into position, her fore-end gently butting the up-hill gates that were closed and waiting. In no time at all I raced up the small lock steps, across the balance beam, and was winding down the paddles on the heavy black gates that I'd closed behind me.

Locks are impressive when you're inside, especially when you're going up hill and staring up at vast brick walls covered with sticky green slime. Sometimes really pretty little ferns grow in the bricks near the top and lower down, lichens and things. It's like being in a secret garden, one that almost nobody sees. Locks are often weird-looking. They come in all shapes and sizes and they can become very slippery. You soon learn to respect them. It's second nature to take great care.

Working locks on your own is very hard work. I ran round with my windlass to wind up the paddles on the top gates. When the paddles were opened and the water gushed in, it seemed to boil with excitement. As the water rushed into the lock I scrambled down the steps and prepared to hop on to *Brigantia* to control the ropes that would hold her steady as we rose.

I know I didn't slip! One minute I was on the steps on the edge of the lock, the next I was somehow wedged in the narrow gap between boat and wall. Rising water was pouring into the lock and gushing and frothing all around me. I was too busy to be frightened. I was cold and wet and drowning. Desperately I tried to free myself, but my body was trapped, held down, it felt, not by the boat but by fingers of steel. My head was bleeding but, strangely, there was no pain. As I blacked out, the last thing I was aware of was the sensation of being violently sucked beneath the tumbling water as the frothing foam rushed rapidly over my head.

At first Brigid felt no lightness in her soul. She clung to the limbs that were shaking her into wakefulness, all but dragging them down with her. She rose wearily from the depths of the river, and as she rose her skin turned to silver, a silver as brittle as her painted-on smile.

It seemed that since time began she had searched the endless rivers. She had walked the centuries until her feet were shredded from the effort, until her heart had been so heavy with hopelessness that Nodens had called her back to the black depths of oblivion, only to rest, rest, rise and search again.

# 4  The rescue

It was the dawn of All Souls' Day so I was sure I must be dead. Someone strange had her arms wrapped round me. Her skin looked as silver as water shining in the light of the moon. I wondered if she was an angel taking me to heaven.

'Am I dead?'

'You're more alive than me,' the apparition said as we clambered inelegantly up the side of the lock. I wasn't sure who was the rescuer and who the rescued. She looked as shaken as me.

'Who are you?' I asked.

My angel was oddly dressed. Her tunic looked simple at first. I could tell it was made of fine bleached linen. Later, when the sun shone, I could see it was woven through with fine strands of gold. Her arms were bare except for knob-ended bangles. She saw my stare . . .

'They're torcs, made of finest gold to show my importance.'

13

I grimaced. I not only had an angel, I had a snobby one. As I shivered uneasily I found myself staring at the gold and silver sunwheel that hung round her long, delicate neck.

'How strange, I've got one of those,' I said, pointing to my sweat-shirt, where a vibrant orb hung suspended in a twisted ring of shiny golden spokes. They twined in plaited threads to the outer edge of the wheel, where they folded over to merge with the outer ring of gold.

'Of course you have. Now, what's the date?' I noticed my angel had no sign of wings and her eyes, a sort of see-through green, were strangely compelling.

'The first of November.'

'Ah, Samhain. The perfect day to rise.'

I gaped at her. She threw her head back and laughed out loud, a rippling laugh, as light as trickling water. 'Do you know, I was beginning to think I'd never rise again. I've been cradled in that murk for absolute centuries. I'm never sure which is worse, endlessly sleeping or endlessly searching.'

I rubbed my head. It was still bleeding so I wasn't dead. I knew I wasn't mad. That only left being ill. I stared at her in silence.

'Where are we? And how far are we from Lydney Sands?' she asked.

I stared at the blood on my fingers. Maybe she was as muddle-headed as me. I looked out across the river. We could have been anywhere. The towpath was deserted except for one or two fishermen. In the far distance a thin man walked a gawky dog. On either side fields stretched for miles until hidden by autumn-dressed woods.

'We're not far out of Windsor,' I said.

'Where are you going?'

'Abingdon.'

'That's miles from the River Severn, isn't it?'

'Yes,' I said cheerfully, 'miles. And just past Abingdon is Oxford, and at Oxford I turn round and come back.'

'Always?' the girl asked, eyeing me curiously.

'Always,' I told her firmly. 'Now, what about you?'

'I'm Brigid,' the stranger told me proudly. 'My name has nothing to do with the fire goddess Brigid either, just in case that's what you're thinking. I am called Brigid in honour of the goddess Brigantia. What's your name?'

'My boat's called *Brigantia*,' I wrapped my tongue proudly round the words. 'And my name's Gwen. Don't you think she's beautiful?'

'The boat *Brigantia*,' Brigid repeated, nodding and sounding really excited, 'and Guendoloen, you are named Guendoloen! I knew Samhain was a good day to rise. I told him! Samhain, I said, next time let it be Samhain.'

I glared at her. The cold must have chilled her brain. 'I am Gwen, simply Gwen.'

Brigid tossed her head. Her golden hair shone pink in the

light of the dawn. 'You are Guendoloen, and anything but simple.'

Brigid and I stared uneasily at one another for a while. She was tall and delicately boned, but I knew she was strong enough to edge *Brigantia* away from the lock wall, strong enough to rise from the depths somehow and push my gashed head clear of water and boat so I could live to work the cut as before.

I smiled at her, unsure what to do next. She read my mind and gave me an impish grin. 'Well, I rescued you, didn't I? Now do your bit, invite me aboard.'

I wanted to say, why? I wanted to say thank you. I did neither. I stepped aside as if she *did* have every right to enter my home, my own private world.

I have no idea why I just let her hop aboard, especially as I knew, even then, that once she stepped foot on *Brigantia* things would never ever be the same.

I let Brigid enter the cabin first. I let her choose my favourite place to sit. I even forgot my bleeding head and made her hot sweet tea. It was as if I had no choice.

Brigid behaved normally enough. She took off her wet clothes and draped them with mine round the stove to dry. Warmly wrapped in blankets, she clutched her steaming mug of tea and gazed round, admiring the gleaming brass ornaments on the tiny shelf and the huge shiny knobs that adorned the brass rail by the cabin door.

I looked at my arms, brown from wind and sun. Her limbs were pale, silver even. I guessed she must usually wear another tunic, a longer one, with sleeves, to protect her limbs from the autumn chill.

'Would you like to borrow a pair of jeans?' I asked. 'And a jumper?'

Brigid shook her head. 'I'll stay as I am, thanks. That tunic will dry in no time.'

'Trousers are more practical. If you stay, you'll have to run across locks all the time and tug canvas sheeting about when we load and unload stock.'

Brigid stared coolly at my gently steaming clothes. 'Right logos, right make of jeans. Go on, admit it, your clothes make you at peace with your time. Well, so do mine. That dress is *me* and I won't change it.'

'I was worried about your modesty and your body temperature, not your street cred,' I told her, only just resisting the urge to punch her snobby little nose. 'My clothes aren't special. The sunwheel sweat-shirt was a leaving present from Mum and Dad, not even a good one. We sell hundreds. Nobody but a tourist would willingly wear one at all!'

'It has no meaning for you then?' she asked, suddenly dropping her head like a sun-wilted flower.

'No!' I said, feeling guiltily pleased to be upsetting her. 'It means nothing at all. It's just a working sweat-shirt. Its only attributes are it's clean and warm, or was until I ended up to my neck in the lock.'

Brigid sighed, 'Yes, I forgot. The sunwheel would have no meaning for you. It's not only Nodens who sleeps.'

'What? Who?'

Brigid shrugged and grinned, 'You'll see. Now our clothes are dry, put on that sweat-shirt again and watch it shine.'

'Those clothes can't be dry!'

'Feel them.'

Brigid was right. I dressed swiftly, trying to block out the thought that it was impossible for clothes to dry so quickly in November, even by the heat of the stove.

'Look, now.'

I opened the narrow cupboard that held all our family's personal things, and dragged out our only mirror. It was right at the back. I think it was only Mum who used it. I stared at my reflection in amazement. The gash on my head had totally vanished!

'My head . . .'

'It hasn't hurt you for ages,' Brigid told me calmly. 'It was only a scratch.'

'It wasn't!' I retorted, even though I was becoming less and less convinced. 'It was deep and it hurt.'

'Well it doesn't now,' Brigid said, grinning, 'so what's the problem?'

I studied myself in Mum's mirror. My face was clean, the blood and all the mud from the lock were gone, there was *no sign* of a gash. I checked my clothes which had been hung but not scrubbed. There was no sign of the blood that had poured so freely from my head. I was neat and tidy and totally healed, and the sunwheel shone. I rubbed my head again but the only thing I felt was confusion. 'How did you do that?'

Brigid threw back her head and laughed. 'I'm a never-born goddess, I have the power . . .'

'Oh spare me!'

'If you don't believe me, look at your sunwheel,' Brigid said, so I did.

The great orb in its centre was radiating a strange light, shimmering really brightly. As I gazed into its centre I imagined I saw a woman's face. The face split slowly into three, merged gradually back to one, then faded gently away. I stood gawping into the mirror until the sunwheel had dimmed back to boring.

'See,' Brigid said, her smile stretching from ear to ear. 'I told you you were anything but simple.'

# 5 Strange company

I have to say that sometimes, just sometimes, I am inclined to believe Brigid is a goddess. She looks frail but she has all the determination of a raging thunderbolt. I've sold everything, absolutely everything, even the sunwheel sweat-shirts and T-shirts, in November! That's never happened before. It was even more incredible because it rained solidly for five whole days. We pulled endlessly at the heavy sodden canvases, turning them backwards and forwards as quickly as possible in order to snatch the goods we wanted at each stop before all our stock was ruined.

Our tempers were beginning to run as high as the waters of the cut. We had just finished dealing in Maidenhead and our next big stop, Reading, was still miles away.

'Can't you do something?' I taunted. 'You're supposed to be the water goddess!'

'I would,' Brigid snarled, 'but that dog of yours is useless at the moment. What power has he against the might of Taran?'

'Den's a dog!' I retorted, not even bothering to ask about Taran. 'What do you want him to do, leap into the air and turn off sky taps with his teeth?'

'Something like that!' Brigid muttered.

'You can't blame the rain on Den,' I said defensively, stroking his head. 'You're supposed to be the one with the power, you do something!'

Brigid let go of the tiller and raised her hands to the sky. I grabbed the tiller as the swirling waters of the usually quiet cut dragged us rapidly towards the stone-walled edges. 'Who do you think you are, King Canute?'

Brigid ignored me and, even worse, when she thought I wasn't looking, she nudged Den determinedly with her foot. Den gave Brigid a reproachful look and shook some excess rain from his coat. Brigid, unimpressed, fixed him with her steely green stare. Den cowed, his tail drooped and he held his head low.

'Brigid!'

'Go and put the kettle on. This business is between Nodens and Taran. It's nothing to do with you and me.'

'Who?'

'Oh, never mind.' Brigid suddenly looked shifty. 'Now,

please, Guen, hot steaming tea. I'm frozen half to death.'

Feeling a bit like a sulky slave, I set the kettle to boil. Brigid stood outside, arms aloft, as if pleading to the storm-laden sky. Black clouds tumbled together. It was so dark it was difficult to see anything except big, black, thundery shapes. I peered out uneasily, watching in amazement as the large black clouds above Brigid slowly took the form of two huge fighting dogs. 'Brigid, look!'

Brigid said nothing but her eyes, like mine, stared fixedly at the sky. The snarling dogs became giant warriors clutching shields in one hand and swords in the other. As their swords locked, lightning flashed and thunder roared. Brigid raised her arms holding up her sunwheel, as if in silent prayer, and moments later the clouds simply merged back into dark smudgy shapes.

I shook myself back into reality, ashamed of my wild imaginings. It was a storm, nothing more. 'Brigid come in at once! You'll get pneumonia.'

Much to my surprise, Brigid shrugged and did as she was told.

'Where's Den?' I asked.

'Den?' Brigid queried, sounding a mite too innocent.

'Den, the wet thing you were kicking just now!'

'Nudging, not kicking,' Brigid said, accepting her tea. 'He's about somewhere, I guess. You know what dogs are like. You just can't rely on them.'

She had that look on her face. I didn't believe a word of it. I grabbed a torch and searched *Brigantia*. There was no sign of Den. I even searched the towpath. Soaked to the skin again, I crept back to the cabin.

'Did you find him?' Brigid asked, her face all false concern.

'No, Den's not here,' I replied, feeling even more miserable.

'He's still got a little business to attend to, I expect,' Brigid said, sounding quite cheerful now the sky was beginning to lighten. 'I'm sure he'll be back soon.'

I cut the engine and tied up *Brigantia*. Brigid scowled. 'I told you, he'll be back soon. Now, start her up. We can't waste time.'

'No! Den's not here, and we need him. He's part of the crew.'

'And up 'til now he's been a fairly useless part,' Brigid said acidly. We glared at one another but in the end we had to laugh, and as we laughed the sun broke through, the rain stopped and Den returned, eyes bright and head and tail held high.

The weather stayed clear, so we made one more drop before lunch and sold loads. 'See, we've done really well,' Brigid crowed triumphantly.

'We'll have to up our order,' I told Brigid as I examined our almost empty hold. 'That's good.'

'You sold them with my help, Guendoloen . . . that's *serious* favours you owe me.'

'I'm not Gwendolen. I'm Gwen!'

'Whoever!' Brigid muttered impatiently. 'Now it's your turn to help me. Equal partners, that's what we agreed. We have to go right across country. We need to reach Lydney and it's very important we get there soon.'

'It's almost winter and I've never been that far before. Lydney's in Gloucestershire,' I told her, sounding more nervous than I cared to admit.

'Would it be easier to travel if the weather was more like summer?' Brigid asked, gazing once more at the sky.

I nodded. The question didn't surprise me. Brigid was a strange girl even though she could haul tarpaulins as well as me. She wore only her fine linen shift, which never creased, tore, looked grubby or stayed wet. Her nails were long and tapered despite shifting grimy sacks. Her ability to stay clean was inhuman.

'So, why do you want summer, exactly?' Brigid pursued as she fingered her necklace.

'In winter the waters run higher, that's good, but in summer we can trade as we pass, and that brings out the tourists we need to earn money to buy food and fuel. We'll need an awful lot of diesel. The journey is much more pleasant in summer. Frozen fingers get sore so quickly,' I said, staring at my chilled chapped hands.

'Would a warm November help?'

'Only a very warm one.'

Brigid looked extremely thoughtful as she stared up at the sky. There was nothing to see but I still felt uneasy. I grabbed Den and shut him safely up in the cabin.

'Stop the boat,' Brigid ordered an hour or so later.

'What now?' I asked. We had almost reached Reading yet there was nothing to see except the endless miles of sleepy fields and hedges that separated us from the bordering towns. The day was cold despite the appearance of a watery sun. The towpath was empty. Even the gongoozlers had long ago returned to huddle by their hearths.

'Now!'

Instinctively I obeyed. I cut *Brigantia*'s engine and let her drift. Brigid went up to the fore-end of the narrow-boat. I followed.

Brigid stood, quietly waiting.

'What are you doing?'

'I'm asking the sky god to help us.'

'The what?'

'Oh, shut-up, Guendoloen! Either go inside or watch quietly.'

Brigid turned her back to me. She positioned herself so she faced the spot where the reluctant sun hovered at its highest point in the sky for the day. I edged round to get a better view. Brigid closed her eyes for a while. Her silver-sheened skin seemed to shimmer slightly. Suddenly she took off her sunwheel and raised it to the sky. The clingy grey clouds turned whiter, as if by command. A single sunray struck the gently swinging sunwheel. I felt a strange warmth, which increased as more rays opened out. The temperature rose steadily, the clouds vanished. My mouth dropped open.

'Did you really do that?' I asked. 'And if so, how?'

Brigid held up her sunwheel, it was spinning rapidly . . . backwards. 'I told the sky god we need the sun if we are to succeed. I told him it was the only way we could reach Lydney Sands in time.'

'And now you've told Jupiter Optimus Maximus Tanarus the weather will be warm as summer,' I said sarcastically.

Brigid nodded, she even had the decency to look impressed. 'Jupiter Optimus Maximus Tanarus, eh? And I thought Tanarus would do!'

'Yep,' I said proudly. 'I told you I liked reading the old stuff. Everything got all mixed up. Tanarus is the celticized form of the Roman name. Zeus, Tanarus, Jupiter – your sky god is them all.'

'No,' Brigid said softly, 'they are all him.'

It became warm; it was chance, these things happen. Brigid was obviously out of her tree. Nobody believes in the old Romano-Celtic gods any more, nobody. But the funny thing was, from that moment on the sun continued to shine.

'Why must we go to Lydney, anyway?' I asked, as I listed all the things we would need to pick up to replace our stock. One bit of me was excited, one bit reluctant. She'd saved my life, she was making me money, Dad would be pleased. I felt I owed her . . . but Lydney was so *far*.

'It's a long story . . .' I groaned but Brigid ignored me. 'The river you know as the Severn was given to Habren. The river was named after her long, long ago. *You* should know that.'

'Why should I?' I asked, and Brigid gave me a long hard look that was totally lost on me. I did know, but for some reason, I didn't want to admit it.

'Over time the River Habren became known as the Sabren, then Sabrina, all thanks to the Romans,' Brigid continued, looking irritable. 'Finally it became the Severn.'

'Yes, so?'

'So, Lydney Sands lies on the River Severn and I must go there to see my father. What's more, it's vital we get there in time.'

'In time for what?'

'Never mind what! You wouldn't believe me if I told you,' Brigid said huffily. 'Just take it from me, it's important.'

'But my work's important too. I need to send money to Mum and Dad. They need it to care for Grandad. That's why we have to sell not only everything from spare machinery to toilet paper and baked beans, but tourist stuff – books, model barges, postcards, T-shirts. We have to trade with the waterside shops to survive.'

'No, we have to go, time is running out. All the other things will work out . . . I promise.'

'I'm not sure the canal system goes as far as Lydney,' I told Brigid desperately. 'Bits of it have been decayed for ages.'

'It doesn't make any difference, we'll find a way.'

'How?'

Brigid laughed and tapped the side of her nose. 'I told you, I am of the water, both of us are, you'll see.'

'I don't want to go!' I said crossly. 'And it's my boat. *Brigantia* is mine.'

'Look here, Guendoloen . . .'

'Gwen!'

'Look here, Guen, I saved your life, didn't I? I sold your stupid stock, didn't I?' Reluctantly I nodded. 'Well then, you have no choice. *You* accompany *me.*'

'What if Mum and Dad come back? They'll be so worried.'

'They won't, I promise. Now stop wimping, Guendoloen, and trust me.'

The trouble was, I didn't. I had this deep, uneasy feeling in the pit of my stomach. The same one that had welled up intermittently since Hallowe'en. I jumped to shore glad I had to run to lock-wheel. I needed to escape Brigid's determined glare. I took my time, pretending the paddles were stiff and difficult to handle. Brigid simply smiled as she leaned on the tiller, quietly waiting.

'You sell books about the olden times, don't you?' she said when I returned, as if our argument was totally forgotten.

I nodded, not admitting them to be my favourites.

'So you know all about us, then?'

I hedged. 'Tales of ancient times are boring, except for the giants, that is. I like them. You're supposed to be Celtic, aren't you?'

Brigid laughed. Her whole face sparkled like raindrops in the sun. 'I knew you would begin to remember, but I am not Celtic. However, I am one of the goddesses best known in the time of the Keltoi. It was Habren who was the Celt, it was Habren.' Her face turned black as thunder. 'I was never born, you see, and why was I never born? Can you remember why, Guendoloen?'

Brigid sounded really menacing now. I was pleased to feel Den rub himself against my legs, pleased to hear him growl softly, as if warning her to tread carefully.

'I've told you again and again, I'm Gwen, nothing to do with your stupid Gwendolen!' I said, sounding more defiant than I felt.

Brigid ignored me, but she'd spotted how sharp Den's bared teeth looked and she backed just a little further away. 'I was not born, Guendoloen, because you had a mind to murder, that's why!'

I stared at her. She was totally mad. I'd never been much further than the end of the towpath. I'd never made a friend, let alone an enemy, so how could I be guilty of murder?

Brigid was smiling again, but now her eyes held an icy

glint. She was playing me, like an otter too full to be bothered to kill his fish. I wanted to push her away yet I wanted her to stay. I felt excited, hooked, as if now was the moment I had waited for all my life.

'We are going to search for the goddess Coventina. She is the goddess of the healing water springs. She's a triple goddess like Brigantia. Both Coventina and Brigantia have three facets and three faces, but with Coventina I know only one . . . mother.

'To wake a triple goddess there have to be the three of us: you, me and Habren. Only when we three are together can my mother, Coventina, rise up once more . . .'

'Absolutely!'

Brigid's eyes narrowed but she still carried on. 'Habren has to be raised so that I can I live and you can be forgiven. Only then will the new millennium be born, and *that's* only if we can wake everybody up in time.'

'Are you absolutely crazy?' I asked, gazing into her bright green eyes. 'You're a book short of a set, you are, a stack short of a tower.'

'I tell you, Guendoloen . . .'

'Gwen!'

'I tell you, Guendoloen, we have work to do. Without us the new millennium is doomed.'

I shrugged. I wanted to say, What's a new millennium but a load of fuss and fire-crackers, a load of noughts in a number?

But Brigid's face was deadly serious. I chickened out. It's hard to be flippant when chilly green eyes are boring into you as they speak avidly of Habren, and at the same time half-blind you with hate.

# 6 Rules for
# the journey

'I'm in charge now,' Brigid said, as we arrived at Reading Junction.

'Look, we *can't* take the Kennet and Avon Canal. We just have to stop at Abingdon, and that's on the outskirts of Oxford. I must restock to pay for the diesel, the canal tolls, the food – everything we need for your precious journey. We'll go up country from here. We'll use the River Thames to Lechlade, then we'll go cross country and aim for the Thames and Severn Canal.'

I tried to sound convincing. I knew the way to Oxford but I'd never been further than that. I remembered old George Cutler rambling to Dad and me about the olden times. He'd said that bits of the Thames and Severn were long since gone, destroyed one way or another by the men who owned the railways, so I didn't think for a moment that we'd get very far. I offered Brigid my brightest smile.

'There's no time to be wasted, Guendoloen. Habren must wake on time . . .'

'We *have* to go via Abingdon,' I repeated crossly. 'They're expecting me to collect. The load's ordered and paid for. We're regulars. If I don't appear, Enid and John will be really worried. They'll write to Mum . . .'

Brigid sighed heavily, 'Guendoloen, you promised!'

'After Abingdon I'll be ready. I'll tell Enid and John that you've hired out the boat for a while, and they'll tell the world, but . . .'

'Ye gods!' Brigid hissed. 'I knew there'd be another "but".'

'But you'll still have to act as a proper crew. There should be three of us really. One to steer, two to open locks quickly so the boat doesn't have to stop more than necessary. Two is slow, two is hard work and you're talking of a very long journey. We have to go up to Lechlade, then across country, through Cirencester and Stroud and then on all the way to Framilode. Maybe we can reach the Severn there, or maybe we'll have to go down the Gloucester and Berkeley Ship Canal until we can cross. I've never been that far, I don't know how the route works.'

'It will work,' Brigid said firmly, 'and I can work. I can do anything.'

'I believe you,' I told her, honestly for once, 'but we have to pull as a team.'

'I can work with you, Guen, I promise.'

I shrugged, she was trying hard, calling me Gwen, but Brigid would say anything to make sure I went with her. She was wearing her best grovelly look and holding up her sunwheel which was still spinning backwards.

'Don't tell me! We're all being ordered about by that thing?' To my amazement Brigid nodded, her face flooding with relief because she thought I understood. I didn't bother to disillusion her. 'Anyway, how come you didn't call me Gwendolen?' I teased.

'Because I can't work with Guendoloen,' Brigid confessed, her look a little sheepish. 'I hate Guendoloen. I hate her but I need her to help rescue Habren. I need her . . . I need you . . . well, you'll see.'

'Tell me later,' I told her hastily. '*Brigantia*'s mine, remember that. Whatever happens, I'm still her captain. We do nothing to cause her harm, understand?'

'Yes number one, sir.' To my surprise Brigid curtseyed and offered her hand. I smacked it, modern style, just to annoy her, and although Brigid looked puzzled, she smiled. I smiled back, a real smile, one that showed in my eyes. If I was honest I was beginning to feel quite pleased about having her aboard. I'd never had an adventure before and I'd never felt the need for a friend. Brigid wasn't *exactly* a friend, but she felt like she belonged with me.

When we had almost finished topping up the butty at the Abingdon warehouses, Enid handed over three letters to Brigid because I was loaded down with boxes. 'Don't you trust her?' John teased, spotting my anxious glance. He took off his cloth cap and started scratching his head.

Brigid ignored him. I winked because I couldn't wave. 'Would you trust her?'

John shrugged and tugged at his little black moustache. I smothered a grin. Somehow he was looking very old-fashioned that day. 'Well, she does look a bit fancy,' he confessed, and both of us giggled.

If Brigid heard our jibes she chose to ignore them. '*Miss Gwen Ansty*,' she read slowly. 'Gwen, is that you?'

'Of course it is,' I said.

'I thought it was G-u-e-n.' Brigid sounded surprised. 'I think it looks better that way.'

'Well, you would,' I retorted, dumping the boxes into the small space left in the hold. As I grabbed my letters I tried writing out Guen in my head. 'I think Gwen's better,' I said, 'I think Guen looks really odd. A Guen should be holding a spear or a horse or something.'

'How about a child and a wool spindle?' Brigid asked sarcastically.

I ignored her and took a break to read my mail. Grandad was happy but frail. Mum was enjoying having a whole house to herself. She'd even started planting things in the garden.

'Is the garden on a hill?' Brigid asked, reading over my shoulder.

'Yes,' I said. 'It's high up and can be very windy. Why?'

'Just curious. Is the pub where your Dad plays skittles at the top of a hill too?'

'No,' I laughed. 'He has to walk all the way down. He has a beer or two, then he has to climb back up, and by the time he gets to the top he's thirsty again.'

'Seems a funny sort of life to me,' Brigid said, but she sounded cheerful and agreed to walk back across the yard with me so I could leave my letters ready to be posted home.

My heart was light as I popped my letters into the post room. *Brigantia* was loaded to the gunwales and so was the butty. There was enough stock to keep us going for ages and, thanks to Brigid's amazing selling abilities, we were a tidy amount in credit. I picked up a final load of boxes, last minute things like chocolates and toothpaste, and said goodbye to the yard hands. I headed back to *Brigantia* whistling happily.

'No moaning?' Brigid asked. 'Have you remembered your promise?'

'Yep,' I said, 'I think I'm about ready for an adventure.'

Brigid grinned and pursed her lips in an attempt to whistle. 'You can't whistle and laugh!' I told her. 'It's impossible.'

Brigid nodded but it didn't stop her trying. I took her arm and waved goodbye to bustling boaters, barely registering how many there were, how frenetic and cluttered the yard was, how like those times described to me once by old George Cutler.

'See you soon,' I called to Enid and John.

'Yes,' Brigid agreed, 'see you soon . . . I hope.'

'What do you mean, *hope*?' I asked, feeling butterflies leap in my stomach. 'We will come back won't we?'

'Oh yes,' Brigid said, trying unsuccessfully to sound reassuring. 'If all goes well, *we'll* stick about for ever!'

# 7 A change of route

'Are you ready?' Brigid asked impatiently. 'Lechlade here we come!'

'What about my letters!' I exclaimed, panicking as I realised I had no choice. 'Mum and Dad'll be very worried if they don't get a reply to their letters.'

'Your parents won't fret just because you've changed your route. Write one more letter. Tell them I've hired you and you'll be too busy to write. That's almost the truth.'

'Oh yes!' I said sarcastically. 'I'll write, Dear Mum and Dad, There's this friend of mine, a river goddess, who appeared out of nowhere. Well, she wants me to freak off to Lydney Sands to meet her dad. He's a sea god, by the way, related to Poseidon and he's the same as Neptune . . . I think . . .'

Brigid's face still looked normal enough, but I collapsed into giggles. 'Well I can see them believing that!'

Brigid took a deep breath, it was the only sign that she was fast running out of composure. 'Write, Miss Brigid Nodens has hired me to take her to Gloucester. Tell them the money's too good to say no to. Tell them you made the Abingdon stop and did well.'

I picked up my pen. Her version did sound much better than mine. I wrote, *Miss Bridget Nodens*.

Brigid pointed. 'Is that how you write my name?'

'It's the modern version, the one Mum and Dad'll see as normal. You're Bridget, I'm Gwen.'

Brigid shook her head. Her golden hair shone brightly in the sun. 'No, I'm Brigid, always have been, always will be, and you are Guendoloen, but for a while, to keep us both happy, I shall try and remember to call you Guen.'

Brigid sat quietly watching me finish my letter. She even searched out a stamp for me. 'You mustn't worry about your land parents. I've told you, they really won't fret too much. They know you were born a slave to the river. They've always suspected there was a reason for you being found as a baby tangled up in the reeds of the River Thames. They were not that surprised, were they, when you refused to leave?'

'I was *found*?' I asked, aghast. 'You mean I was *adopted*?'

'Of course you were found,' Brigid said, as if that was the best thing that could have happened to me, and not a devastating revelation. 'You were left in a basket tightly woven from living reeds. You were warm and comfortable and in no danger. Your basket nest rested beside a sea of white lilies that just shouted for you to be found. I suppose you're right, you were adopted . . . in a fashion. The only odd thing was that nobody noticed how special you were, so special that the reeds and water lilies round you were in flower out of season.'

'I was found like Moses, I suppose?' I retorted, now more used to her strange imaginings but still not willingly believing a single word.

'No, like Brigantia and Coventina, the goddesses of river and spring. Only, you didn't look like a river goddess, you looked just like a water babe. No one could tell you were born of sinning stock.'

'What rubbish you spout, Brigid!' I screeched, shocked by the very suggestion of being dumped to be raised by strangers. Shocked by the thought that my mum and dad might not be my *real* parents.

'Look, why do you think you weren't registered?' Brigid's eyes glittered like brittle green glass. 'They knew you were born bad.'

'I was not born bad and my parents love me even if I am adopted!' I yelled. 'But I think you're lying! I think they would have *said*!' I lunged at Brigid, preparing to grab her arms and tumble her back into the river she loved to boast about so much.

Brigid held my wrists, her grip solid as steel. 'I told you, you are here for a purpose, my purpose. You have no choice.'

I struggled helplessly. Brigid kept her grip tight but her voice softened. 'Look, your land parents do love you, I know that. They love you very much, Guen. I quite like you, now, in this time and this space.' Brigid sighed. 'But on our journey you must become the Guendoloen of the past even though I hate her.' Brigid relaxed her grasp but kept hold of one of my hands. 'You are the key to my past, and all our futures. You have to believe. You have to live as Guendoloen, feel as Guendoloen, you *have* to remember your roots.'

I felt too shocked to be hurt, too angry to hold on to my disbelief. 'So why, prissy-miss water goddess, Brigid of the water brain, why if you hate me so much, do you insist on keeping me company?'

'Guendoloen, believe me, I need you. You are the key to everyone's happiness.'

'Well, I don't need *you*. I've had enough of your wild tales. Get off my boat. This is my journey.' I held-in *Brigantia*. 'Go! Jump on to the towpath and disappear for ever. Oxford's only five miles back. Go there. If that's too difficult, leap back into your river. Just vanish, will you!'

'I'm sorry, Guen,' Brigid said, sounding strangely contrite. 'I am my father's daughter and my temper runs fast like the racing bore. Please, Guen, let me stay.'

'Is this journey really so important?' I was curious in spite of the alarm bells ringing so loudly in my head.

'It's life and death to me,' Brigid said softly. 'The whole world's in dreadful danger.'

I would have laughed but I knew for sure that she believed every word. I suspected I was out of my mind. I felt like a weak-willed wimp as I stepped back, letting her stand more safely on the gunwale. 'I'll regret this, I'm sure.'

'I don't think so,' Brigid said, half smiling. 'Not in the end.'

# 8  Brigid v Taran

'Horses! Pulling a *barge*! Brigid?'

'It must be for the tourists,' Brigid replied, giving me a suspiciously innocent look.

'I know Lechlade is always full of gongoozlers,' I agreed. 'It's so beautiful here, especially where the River Coln joins the Thames, but it can't be a tourist boat. For a start, tourist boats are almost always narrow-boats, and that's a barge. George Cutler told me that when the boat people dress up they put on their snazziest outfits. Look at this family, their clothes are far too dull and old looking. Also, if that old barge was designed for gongoozlers it would be so bright with roses and castles you'd need sunglasses . . . even in November.'

'Not if they were re-enacting a working-day barge

period piece,' Brigid retorted smugly.

I stared at the boat family. Mother and daughter wore subdued flowery frocks and bibbed white aprons. The mother's dress came down to her ankles and was light green on dusky green. The daughter's had the same sort of cut and flowery pattern but was in shades of sky blue. The father, like his sons, wore brown serge. The material looked rough and so heavy I could imagine it itching against his skin. He had a waistcoat and cap in the same dull tones. The two boys wore grey-and-blue striped jumpers, the sort I vaguely remembered my grandad wearing. They wore shorts that came right down to their grubby knees and long straggly socks that struggled to stay up. 'Whoever willingly dresses like that?' I asked, but Brigid ignored me.

They were behaving normally enough though. The father stood watching the approach of Halfpenny Bridge, his hands resting quietly on the tiller behind him. The mother had gone into the cabin, but then she came back with some boating papers and money for the toll.

'Tolls! See, Brigid, the keeper's cottage is back, they're about to pay a toll! That's a funny looking coin. It looks a bit thick. What is it?'

'It's a ha'penny, that's why it's called Halfpenny Bridge. It's very good acting, isn't it?'

'We haven't got a ha'penny, they're not made any more.'

'Stop worrying, Guen. Forget about the bridge keeper.

He won't show the least bit of interest in us.' To my surprise Brigid was right. As soon as the family had showed him their papers and handed him the coin, he vanished.

One of the boys was leading their old mare along the towpath, the other sat on the cabin roof playing five-stones with his sister.

'You can't get a horse under *there*!' Brigid said, eyeing the dark portals of the approaching bridge.

'No,' I told her, 'the horse would be led over the bridge . . . see the little path over there? That was what it was designed for.'

Brigid and I held-in behind the horse-drawn barge and cut our engines. It was obvious the family would have to leg the barge under the bridge. The father had already laid down clean boards to lie on. Even though it was fairly narrow, the passage through would take some time.

'That's *never* a tourist boat,' I insisted as we watched the boy release the horse from its long harness. 'See, the barge hold's full of steel. Since when did you see a barge carrying steel?'

Brigid didn't answer. She pointed, her mouth dropping in horror. A huge black dog had sprung out of nowhere and was leaping up at the mare. The horse reared, trying to knock the dog down with its hooves. It was neighing in panic. The dog continued to advance, mouth agape. Its huge white teeth shining out like slashing cutlasses as it snarled and snapped and drew ever closer.

The horse stood no chance. Whinnying in terror, it backed again and tumbled straight into the cut, sending vast plumes of water everywhere.

The man swung his tiller, desperately trying to avoid the thrashing mare. I swung ours too, trying to avoid him. The drowning horse was now trapped under the bridge. The frightened children were shrieking in horror. It was awful!

'Don't scream, what good is that? You'll scare Nelly even more,' the father ordered. 'Get to the other side, and hurry!'

The children calmed instantly, soothed by his authority and the possibility of helping. The father handed the barge ropes to his daughter while the rest of the family raced across the bridge.

'It's Taran!' Brigid muttered to herself. 'That Taran is going to be the death of me.'

'Who's Taran?' I called, catching her words, but Brigid was gone.

'Can you tie good knots?' I asked the scared little girl.

'Yes, Miss.'

I threw her our ropes. 'If you tie *Brigantia* up to the horse ring over there by the bridge, I'll try to help.' I raced after the others. The bridge was the width of a narrow road but it seemed to take for ever to get to the other side.

The father had stripped down to his long johns and was desperately swimming towards his frantic horse, dragging the long harness behind him. The mother hung on to ropes pulled through the harness, wildly hoping she and her kids would have the strength to haul their mare through the bridge to safety. The horse was snorting and choking now, her eyes were rolling. It was obvious that she would soon give up her fight for life. There was no way we could back the barge and narrow-boat enough to reach her from the blocked side in time.

'What do you want me to do?' I asked the mother. 'Help you or your husband?'

The mother didn't seem to hear. She looked sick with worry. Man and horse were her life. She watched him trying to calm the now weakly struggling mare, trying to put on the harness, trying not to drown himself, all at the same time. I stood by her side. Seconds seemed to last for ever.

Eventually the man managed to secure the harness and gave the signal to pull. We pulled, all of us, for the youngest child had joined us now, but to no avail. The horse seemed to be stuck in some mud. Her feet thrashed but only her head showed.

'It's no good!' the man yelled. 'The daft bat's stuck fast. She's going to drown.'

We pulled the ropes, using strength that seemed to come from nowhere, but still the horse stayed stuck. I looked round for Brigid. Why wasn't she helping? Where was she?

Suddenly, from the depths of the canal, came a disembodied voice. 'Pull! Pull *now*!'

We made a final effort, every muscle taut and aching. One, two, three . . .

Before our tired eyes the old mare rose up from the water. I tell you, she *rose* out, as if lifted by some giant hand. There was a big slurping sound as her feet were released from the mud and her belly from the water. She whinnied in surprise.

Once more we heaved, and this time she came towards us so easily that we stumbled backwards into the nettles on the bank, adding stings to our muddied bruises. We picked ourselves up and stood in stunned silence. There, on the side of the towpath, stood the barge mare, yet the sides of the cut were high, the water low – there was no way she could have just scrambled out.

The woman pointed to the dripping horse. 'How?'

'I tell you, she flew!' her man said, dragging himself up and over the edge. 'She just *flew*!'

'She couldn't have,' I said, but the family didn't care *how*. They were too busy leading the mare back so they could rub her down to stop her being chilled. She was their livelihood, more important to them than gold. But the little girl suddenly turned back.

'She did fly, Miss, I saw her too.'

'It's a miracle,' I said, smiling back at her. 'I'm so glad she's safe.'

'Thank you! Thank you *and* your friend.'

'Brigid? You saw Brigid?'

The girl giggled. 'Of course I saw her. It was her who lifted Nelly. It was her that made her fly!'

I didn't want to believe her, but Brigid did claim to be a goddess. I remembered the moment I rose from the waters of the frothing lock, my legs gripped by fingers of steel.

I stepped back aboard *Brigantia*. Brigid welcomed me. She looked exhausted but she was clean and smiling.

'Where've you been?' I demanded.

'Here and there. You managed, didn't you?'

'The little girl says she saw you. She says you pushed Nelly up from the mire.'

'Me?' Brigid said, examining her spotless fingers. 'That's the trouble with little children, far too imaginative, don't you think?'

I was too tired to argue. I shrugged.

'Ugh! You're filthy, absolutely disgusting. Drink this and then we'll go over to the bath-house, but we can't dally too much. Because of Taran we've already wasted far too much time.'

'Bath-house?'

'Yep, over there. I'll even hold your towel for you.'

I stared in the direction of her finger. 'That place wasn't there before, I know it wasn't and before we do *anything*, I want to know, who is Taran?'

'Taran is just a dog with no manners,' Brigid said, glaring at Den. 'In the same way that, most of the time, Den is a dog with no brain.'

'No, Den's fine. I like him just as he is.'

'Well, you would!' Brigid muttered, her mood darkening. 'It was your cruelty that destroyed what little brain he had!'

# 9   The fathers' war

'Why are you writing to your mum and dad again?' Brigid asked.

'If I don't, they'll worry about me. That's what parents do, worry.'

Brigid's look told me she thought I was a real fusspot. 'I can't write to mine, even if I wanted to. My father . . .'

'I know! Nodens, the greatest of river gods.'

'Well he was. The Keltoi loved him 'til things went wrong. Now he sleeps in the shifting sands of Lydney.' Brigid sounded really sad. 'The people no longer know him. They no longer bring him offerings to give thanks for healing, or gifts of food and wine to celebrate their harvests. They have forgotten how to call out for help when their men are swept out to sea or when the rivers refuse to give up their fish. They don't even call when their children fall into the river and drown. They have forgotten and he is ashamed. That's why he sleeps.'

'Why should they remember? What's the use of an old river god when we've got a better one, one who can do anything.'

'Look at the rivers drying up. Breathe the pollution in the air. See the land buried in concrete. Your God's more like the creator, so tell me, where are his servants? Where are the earth guardians? Who really cares? Nodens was given only one job, so he could do it better . . .'

'Well he doesn't, not if you are to be believed!'

'For the moment he sleeps,' Brigid said, glaring at me, 'but my father, son of Manannan . . .'

'Your grandfather's who?'

'You might know him better as Neptune, that's his Roman name.'

'Greek, Celtic, Roman, what difference the name?' I asked, trying to irritate her so much she would stop bothering to tell me.

'None whatever,' she continued calmly. 'Anyway, Manannan, my grandfather, was the god of the rivers and the sea until he gave over the rivers. My father, Nodens, took control of them and was especially fond of the River Severn, now Habren's river. He loved that river even more than the Thames. He was pleased to give the river Habren's name so she would never be forgotten, but he's still the power behind its shifting sands and the tumbling bore.'

'He sounds like a bore,' I said, wondering why a permanently sleeping father and a huge rolling wave held such fascination for her.

Brigid read my mind. 'Nodens is my *father*,' she snapped, 'though I admit, he wasn't a terribly good one.'

Who else but Brigid could claim to have river gods for parents? As usual, I humoured her to make life easy, but I have to say I found it hard *believing*. Mind you, if she *really* believed her own yarns, I had some sympathy. I had one God to make me feel guilty; her life must be fraught with danger, because she had whole rivers full to pacify.

'Nodens still is the greatest of river gods,' Brigid said. 'He's kind and generous and good to his people.'

'How can he be if he sleeps?'

'He can take the form of a dog so he can travel about and see what's happening, see what needs to be done, but when he becomes a dog he has to *behave* like a dog. It's dangerous for people to know he's a shape-changer. People panic because they've heard the legends. They know that if he appears as a dog it's important. It means life or death for someone.'

'Fair range of choice then,' I said, eyeing Den curled up asleep on the bow. He looked like a dog, he smelled like a dog. 'So why are you telling *me*?'

'You need to understand the way of the Keltoi, and if I

tell you bit by bit you might come to believe.' Brigid sounded miserable. 'I've never known my father, not as you know yours. I hear his voice echo in the water. I feel his love in the air around me. I know that in spirit he's close, but his body lies miles away.'

'What happened?' I asked, beginning to feel sorry for her. I couldn't imagine life without my dad there to moan at me or gently tease. Corrie *was* my dad, I was sure he was, even if I did spend some time floating about in a basket.

'Nodens lost his temper, such a temper. What can you do if your voice echoes like thunder when you shout, if when you point your finger in anger the lightning has no choice but strike?'

'Keep calm, I suppose . . .'

'He tried, really he did, but if the sky turned black and the waters rose, then the people knew that someone had taken a step too far.'

'I suppose we can all throw a wobbly now and then.'

'What's your dad called?' Brigid asked, and I was shaken, she'd never shown any interest before. I found a stamp and stuck it on my postcard.

'Colin. His name's Colin, but we all call him Corrie because that's what I used to say when I was small.'

'Corrie's a good name. Colin! Well, that's a really stupid name,' Brigid said firmly. 'I can't think why he was called Colin at all.'

I assumed the reason for her rudeness was jealousy, and that every time I wrote a letter or sent a card I was reminding her she walked through life alone.

'Colin's better than Nodens!' I sneered. 'And my dad's better than yours. Your dad does nothing but loiter by rivers chasing women. He keeps his brains . . .'

'How do you know about Nodens?' Brigid asked. She wasn't the least bit angry. She was jumping up and down in excitement. 'How do *you know*, Guen?'

I felt flustered. 'You must have told me.'

'I didn't,' Brigid insisted, 'but as usual you've twisted things. Nodens hasn't looked at another woman seriously, not since he met Coventina.'

I was not impressed. 'My dad met my mum when they were teenagers, at Siddington Lock near Cirencester, the fourth lock in the flight. Dad was enjoying a weekend break fishing and Mum was a gongoozler on holiday. They knew they were right for each other. They fell in love straight away.' I did not let Brigid know that, just as I had suddenly known about Nodens, I was sure Corrie *was* my father, but from another space, another time.

'My mum hooked Corrie with a smile,' I continued, hoping that's who she was, 'and since then Corrie's never even glanced at another woman.'

'Is he blind?'

'No, he's loyal and he's sensible.'

'He sounds very boring to me!' Brigid retorted huffily. 'My dad likes women. He thinks they're too pretty to ignore.'

'He soon ignored Brigantia! He ignored her when he realised that she was far too clever for him!'

'How did you know *that*?' Brigid asked, grinning like a Cheshire cat.

I shuffled and looked down at my feet. 'I don't know, it was just a silly idea that popped into my head. I was being as silly as your father and his dolly birds with rocking-horse brains.'

I watched in amazement as huge tears began to well up in Brigid's eyes, making them look like deep-green crystal pools. 'My dad loves my mum,' she sobbed. 'He always will. My mum is clever. My mum is the best.'

I felt irritation rather than pity. 'She can't be, not if she can't see Nodens for the sex-mad scatterbrain he really is.'

'My dad's lovely,' Brigid whimpered, 'and so is my mum.'

'How do you know? How do you know if, as you say, because of me you were never really born?'

Brigid wiped the tears from her eyes but they only welled up again. I began to feel guilty and ashamed. Why had I felt the need to be so cruel? 'I love my dad too,' I told her gently as I handed her some tissues, 'but you are right, he can be a bit boring. He's like me, happiest doing simple things, like puddling endlessly up and down river and cut.'

'Your dad only took on *Brigantia* for money.'

'I know that! It was the only job going at the time. It was chance, but he gave it his best. He did well.'

'I bet he plods up and down his hill looking for beer well too,' Brigid said, and I was almost relieved to hear her sounding so sarcastic. 'How often does he play Humpty-Dumpty then, Guendoloen?'

'He never gets drunk and he never falls down,' I said, falling neatly into her trap.

'See, my dad's more human than your dad. My dad at least lives life. The most your dad dares is to neglect your mum for an hour or two of an evening. I can't see why he wants to go anyway. My dad never wanted to leave Coventina.'

'My mum doesn't mind,' I insisted. 'She can have the whole cabin to herself, lots of privacy to bathe and wash her hair. She can have an extra kip, a quiet one . . . no snoring. Think, Brigid, for you this is just an interlude, an adventure. *Brigantia* is our world. In bad weather we can be stuck together in this small cabin day after day after day. Everyone needs a little space sometimes.'

'Well, I think your dad's incredibly dull. There's a whole world out there he hasn't seen, a whole lot of life he hasn't tasted. I think you have to make mistakes in life to learn.'

'I haven't made any mistakes, not big ones,' I told Brigid smugly. 'And I don't think I'm boring.'

'Well, you always did see things your way! That's why you found it impossible to see that Estrildis was just one of life's pawns. That's why Habren died before her time and I was never born . . .'

'Estrildis? Habren? I tell you, I know nothing of them!'

'You do! You just *refuse* to remember. Everything happened because you couldn't see further than your smug little nose. You were *evil*, Guendoloen! You wanted revenge and started the bad times. Because of you the Keltoi forgot to nurture the air, earth and water that gave them life, and since then things have slowly gone from bad to worse. Men have become greedy and infertile. Women want everything but can't cope. Every year more children are sick, many of them finding it impossible to breathe. *That's* why you have to remember, that's why you have be present at the end!'

'The end of what?'

'The end,' Brigid said, looking at me as if I was incredibly stupid, 'of this rotten millennium, of course.'

# 10 The evil Taran

'In the beginning there was nothing, absolutely nothing anywhere. Can you imagine nothing?' Brigid asked as she handed
over the tiller so I could manoeuvre us over the Smerrill
Aqueduct. It felt really odd, a canal passing over a valley road.

'Not easily,' I admitted, wondering whether to tell Brigid
to shut up because I knew the creation story, but I ended up
waving to a passing boatie and letting her gab on. If I was
honest, I was beginning to like her exotic tales. They made
the long quiet stretches of water slide past very quickly.

We were across Smerrill Aqueduct and heading towards
Thames Head Bridge before I remembered that it shouldn't
be there. Old George Cutler had once confessed to helping
to destroy Smerrill Aqueduct when the road was widened to

build the railway. I looked back. The aqueduct was gone. I shook my head, not wanting to believe what I saw.

'Are you listening?' Brigid said impatiently. 'There is so little time, and so much for you to learn.'

'Go on,' I said, needing the rhythm of her voice to soothe me back to sanity.

'In the beginning there was nothing, just this great earth tumbling in the empty heavens. No people, just earth, dust and endless winds.'

'So it was after the big bang then,' I said, holding out to position *Brigantia* centrally so we could pass through an approaching bridge hole. I stopped speaking and pointed. A dog was growling at the bridge entrance. I was sure it was the very same dog that had attacked Nelly, the old mare. Den saw him too and leapt on to the bank. I started to shout but Brigid clamped her hands over my mouth.

'Better him than us!' she hissed.

Den approached the black beast, his lips curled back in warning. I'd never ever seen him looking so fierce. His ears were laid flat, his fur stood on end making him seem twice the size, his teeth were bared and dangerous. To my relief the strange black dog simply snarled back before fading into the trees.

Brigid and I relaxed. Den returned and revelled in our praise. 'Our beginning was after the emptiness, if that's what you mean. There were lots of big bangs. The creator commanded the sky god to send down thunderbolts. The water tumbled everywhere, angrily boiling up huge plumes of foam. The sky was alive with lightning. The storm and the earth were in vibrant chaos, there was no control, so the creator reached out and touched the boiling seas and we were born.'

'Who is "we" exactly?' I asked, trying to imagine the delicately formed Brigid controlling or even rising from an angry storm.

'The gods, especially Manannan god of the sea . . .'

'I preferred Neptune . . . hunky man with trident,' I said, but my teasing was lost on her.

'Manannan is the better name, Guen, the *older* name. Manannan and the other gods were commanded to bring order to earth, sea and sky. Taran was supposed to help the sky god, but creating him turned out to be a bad move, a really bad mistake. There's always a worm that turns.'

'I'd guessed that you didn't like him.'

'Didn't like him! I loathe him. Believe me, Guendoloen, Taran always means trouble.'

I stifled a laugh. It wasn't only Taran who was trouble. Here I was, quite calmly steering *Brigantia* along waters I knew no longer existed. Here I was, risking my life and my beautiful boat for a girl who spent half her life hating me, without my even knowing *why*. I was beginning to wonder if Brigid really liked anybody, but she was in full flood so I didn't bother to ask, not about the hate or the bridge or anything.

'My father Nodens controlled the rivers,' Brigid sighed. 'There were so many rivers, and they were so small and so widely distributed that my dad couldn't cope and needed help, so the goddesses Brigantia and Boannan were created to help him and my mother Coventina, who was given charge of the life-giving springs. We, the immortal, were there, right from the start of life. We have been there ever since.'

'Through nothing to blue-green algae?'

Brigid nodded.

'Through fern and dinosaur to Stone Age man?'

'Guendoloen, will you listen! Time is not important. It's very simple. Manannan rules the water. Taran is the link between water and sky and, like Nodens, he can control thunder, and thunder brings rain. The tasks are shared between them just like Coventina, Brigantia and Boannan share rivers and springs.

'Everyone has failings. My father Noden's failing was that he loved looking at pretty girls. Taran's sin was that he needed constant adoration. If the people failed to give him generous offerings when he warned them they were needed by crashing together his great thunderclouds, the sky would be black and angry for days.

'Taran and Nodens were supposed to work together, but they hated each other from the start. Nodens only asked for the best wine to be spilled on his waters, or the freshest flowers strewn. At his healing shrine on Lydney Sands there might be silvered limbs or bronze statues, but he never demanded them. He always said that a simple wooden token worked just as well.'

'Why did Nodens need *any* tokens?' I asked, not willing to show her flashy father too much sympathy.

'The Keltoi had to make offerings to show him where their pain was. They couldn't see him, they couldn't write to him; it was the only way.'

'No human sacrifice ever, then?' I checked.

Brigid gave me a long hard look. I shuffled, not quite sure what she was expecting from me. 'Well?' I asked again.

'Sometimes Nodens took a drowning soul. He *never* asked, but sometimes he accepted the gifts that were offered. He never wasted a soul. It was always rested in the Otherworld so it could be used later for a greater purpose. Taran was the one who loved human sacrifice. He loved to hear people screaming as their souls were wrenched from their burning flesh. Taran encouraged people to stuff human offerings into the trunks of hollowed-out oak trees, so they could be slowly burned alive even though they were never needed. Imagine slowly burning someone alive, Guendoloen? Taran was, and is, especially evil.'

'So is Taran still about?' I remembered the fighting dog clouds and knew that he was.

'Not knowing the depravity of Taran, the creator blamed

the Keltoi for the killings. He decreed a storm,' Brigid continued, trying hard not to be fazed by my constant interruptions. 'He said the people had sinned and because of that they must die, all except Noah who, it is said, was a man above men . . .'

'The biblical Noah?'

Brigid shrugged. 'Noah's just a name, it's what he represents that counts. We are all reborn to travel the circle of time. Anyway, there were huge amounts of water cascading down from the heavens. Vast seas were created in days, everyone was kept busy, people and gods . . . especially Taran. The people were scared rigid by a sky where night was bright as day, lit by bolts of lightning that set fire to their fields even though it rained. They were deafened by thunder, frozen by water. They did the only thing they thought would appease, they burned hundreds more of their people.

'The stench was so bad that Manannan looked up from his oceans and Tanarus, the sky god, peered out through the clouds. The two gods wondered what the people were up to. The sky god took the form of an eagle and flew over the burning pyres. Manannan became a humble frog and hopped so close it was easy to hear.

'The eagle flew over the huge tree-trunks and heard the terrified screams of the dying. "Help! Help!" they called, but only Tanarus the eagle seemed to care.

' "Why do they burn?" asked the eagle.

'The people replied, "Taran the storm god commands. Every year he takes more and more of us." '

' "Why do you hollow such big holes in the oak?" Manannan the frog asked the workers who toiled in the forests.

' "Because Taran commands," replied the labourers, "and we are afraid to disobey, for Taran says the day we fail, all of the people will die." The eagle and the frog went to village after village and the questions and answers were always the same.'

'How come the creator didn't know what was going on?' I asked.

'He did, that was why he ordered the flood, to stop the burning of men, but because he'd been kept busy recycling the souls of the dead, he missed the fact that the instigator was Taran. The creator was absolutely furious when he learned the truth. He aimed a huge spike of lightning straight at Taran. It struck Taran full in the face, instantly blinding him. At the same moment, Manannan sent up a great wave, a breaker so tall it reached the skies. Taran couldn't see the danger. When the surge hit him he stumbled and tumbled. The wave sucked him into its depths and he drowned.'

'Another anti-hero gone for ever,' I said, wondering if the black dog would appear when we reached Sapperton Tunnel.

'There was no chance Taran would sleep for ever but, for the moment, the creator was satisfied. The sea calmed and the sky turned blue. Noah stopped feeling seasick and started to look for land. After that, everything was fine. Fine, that is, until you were born! Because of you, Guendoloen, we were all swept into the waters of oblivion.'

'Hey, that's a bit strong. I'm not yet sixteen and I've lived all my life on river and cut. How can I have changed your world?'

'OK, not you, perhaps,' Brigid admitted grudgingly, 'but your past self, the original self, Guendoloen, Queen of the Celts.'

I shivered, feeling a strange cold sensation running up and down my spine. Guendoloen, always we came back to Guendoloen.

'So where does Habren come in?' I asked, holding in *Brigantia* so we were positioned ready to enter the next lock.

Brigid opened her mouth but I slowed the engine and handed her the tiller. 'Later, keep *Brigantia* moving steadily while I lock wheel.'

I picked up the windlass and jumped on to the towpath, racing up river to prepare the next lock gates so that when *Brigantia* caught up she could gently slide in.

I was back in my world, a world that to me was both safe and solid. I cranked open the paddles feeling a quiet satisfaction as the water levelled under my control. I felt no fear of slipping as I ran from one side to the other, across the narrow tops of the gates. I felt more and more sure that it wasn't carelessness that had hurled me that day into swirling waters. It was something else, something mystical. Steel fingers had pushed me, sucked me under, almost drowning me, but if those fingers belong to Brigid, why?

# 11 Shadows of fear

November had turned into December and still the sun shone brightly. I looked longingly at the lay-by at King's Reach just before the Coates end of Sapperton Tunnel. 'Can't we stop here? We could go and look at Coates roundhouse. I'd love to go there. It was the lengthmen's cottage. We could have lunch at Tunnel House, imagine that! That's where the men in charge of the horses used to rest up while the leggers took the boats through the tunnel. In the old days it could take five hours to leg your way through Sapperton Tunnel if you were going against the flow.'

'I tell you, Guen, there's no time.'

Reluctantly I centred *Brigantia* ready to enter the dark bridge portal. As I looked up I noticed the empty niches in the facing wall. Brigid's eyes followed my gaze. 'Do you know whose statues should have gone in there?' she asked.

I racked my brains. I knew George Cutler had *said* . . . 'Old Father Thames was one.'

'Quite right!' Brigid said, sounding a bit too enthusiastic. 'And who is Old Father Thames?'

I put my fingers to my lips and pretended to be deep in thought. 'No, don't tell me, it's coming, yes I'm sure now. Old Father Thames was Nodens. Yes, I'm sure that's who he was.'

While Brigid was still looking pleased, I handed her the tiller so I could check all our lanterns were functioning properly. 'Don't move it. You'll get the urge to swing her round, you'll feel like the boat is spinning in circles. Don't compensate, hold her steady unless I call to you. It's an illusion. The brain goes funny for a while when you go from bright light to pitch dark.'

I poled the sides of the bridge checking for obstructions. 'Brigid, you know this is a waste of time. Sooner or later we'll have to stop.'

'Was Smerrill a waste of time? We go on, we have no choice.'

I glanced back at Coates entrance. All I could see was a small circle of light in the gloom. 'Move that tiller about two degrees left, then hold her steady again.' I stood at the leading edge of *Brigantia*, nervously poking at the tunnel walls. No trouble so far. For a while we worked in silence and all that

69

could be heard was the low rumble of the engine. The sound bounced off the enclosing walls becoming more and more oppressive. Light from our lamps struck erratically at the damp arch above us. Dancing shadows leaped about. They seemed to grow ever larger, ever more threatening.

'I'm scared,' Brigid confessed. 'I hate going back into the dark.'

'I'm scared too, but more for my boat than me.'

'You have no faith in this journey, that's your trouble. *Brigantia*, at least, is safe.'

'How do you know?' I picked up a lantern so I could see her face.

'Old Father Thames was one of those statues,' Brigid said, her face pale and anxious in the darkness. 'The other was Lady Sabrina.'

'Lady Sabrina!'

'Lady Sabrina, the name Habren came to be known by. Habren, Sabren, Sabrina, Severn – remember?'

'But why here, and why were they never erected?'

'Where better than here, a point close to the spring of the rising Thames and en route to the Severn. This was a place Nodens and Coventina knew well, believe me.'

'Yes, if this tunnel had been here it would have come in really handy,' I said sarcastically. 'Fancy you being afraid of the dark.'

'I am not afraid of the dark,' Brigid said crossly. 'I am afraid of going back to the dark. I have spent so much time waiting for the chance to go towards the light, and now we have very little time to make things right.'

'So why were the statues never put into the niches?' I asked, poking at the crumbling brickwork. It wasn't good but, to my relief, it still held.

'Nodens wouldn't have it. Every time the statues were put into the niches he tumbled them into the cut. He felt ashamed. He didn't want the people to have a reminder of his darkest day.'

I shrugged and went back to checking the tunnel walls. They were getting softer. I slowed our engine almost to a stop and went back to check again. I held my pole right out in front of *Brigantia*, desperate to save her from damage.

Brigid sensed change too. She watched me anxiously as I poled the walls round us. 'It's totally blocked ahead. We have to go back.'

'Not a chance. We *have* to go on.'

I ignored her and pushed my pole into the fallen wall edging us quietly backwards. 'It's a pity, we were almost through.' As if to prove me right, the huge stone I kept pushing dislodged enough to reveal a narrow tunnel through the debris. Brigid and I peered through. We could clearly see the cut running into the bend on the other side. 'So near and so far,' I said, feeling really sorry for her.

'Push *Brigantia* backwards!'

'You said . . .'

'Just do it, as quick as you can!'

As I poled us backwards as fast as I could, I sensed rather than saw Brigid pull the sunwheel from her neck and hold it high in her free hand. It began to glow in the dark, giving even more life to the vibrantly dancing shadows. I felt very scared as I continued to pole. Every muscle in my body ached. Eventually I ran out of breath and had to stop.

'Look!' I said, peering through the small hole in the wall. Brigid ignored me. She gripped the sunwheel, her eyes shut as if in prayer.

A ball of orange-yellow light appeared in the waters of the cut. It looked like a bold reflection of the setting sun until it began to move towards us, bigger brighter faster. I realised it was travelling just *above* the water. I gulped in horror. Coming towards us at high speed was a huge frightening fireball.

'BRIGID!'

'Duck!' Brigid ordered. 'And for goodness sake close your eyes!'

I ducked. Never have I ducked faster. The ball of fire drew so close I was sure I would be toasted, but the shimmering orb passed over my head, over *Brigantia*, and on towards Coates portal.

'Ye gods!' Brigid said. 'That was close!'

I scrambled back up on to my feet. 'What was that?'

'Ball lightning,' Brigid said, grinning. 'Nodens got his act together for once, he must have pinched it from Taran.' I was so relieved to be safe I had *no trouble* believing her.

'What now?' I asked, for although there was now a huge hole to pass through, we were surrounded by enormous tumbled rocks and there was debris everywhere. I took the lantern and nervously checked *Brigantia* all over. 'She's OK,' I said, surprised. 'But how can we move on?'

Brigid smiled and pointed.

One moment I could see Den, oblivious to the chaos, standing on the cabin roof wagging his tail proudly as if he was the pilot, the next he seemed to grow into the blackness round us. I held my lantern high and, before my very eyes, Den's shadow slowly took the form of a giant of a man. I watched, too startled to speak, as he held up the crumbling roof in his immense hands. Where piles of stone blocked our way he casually scooped them up, clearing our path and dropping the debris behind us. If I hadn't felt the drips of water as the handfuls of wet rock passed over us, or heard the splashing as the rocks settled behind us, I would never have believed.

'Did you see that, Brigid?'

'I saw only dancing shadows, didn't you?'

'No, I saw a ball of fire. I saw someone save us. I . . .' Brigid was laughing her head off, she wrapped her arms round me and gave me a proper loving hug. 'I know what you saw, silly, I was *teasing*.'

# 12 Goemagot

'Not long before Habren was born,' Brigid said, handing me the tiller so I had to stay, 'this land was ruled by giants. The most famous one being King Albion who ruled for many peaceful years. Great Britain was called Albion then in honour of him.'

I stared at Brigid uneasily. I remembered reading the story of the giants, I remembered the running sea of their dying blood. I found myself shivering as I pooped our horn before manoeuvring us safely through the next bridge hole. I pretended to be too busy to listen, but Brigid just yapped on.

'Some of the original giants were the sons of demons and they mated with the husband–slaying daughters of Daocletian.'

Now I could laugh! 'Really, Brigid, whatever will you think of next, people the size of peas? Man eating toads?'

'Don't mock, Guendoloen. This is your past, your history. Albion was killed by Brut and Corineus. They killed king and country, they changed everything.'

I shrugged.'Look at that sky!' I said to distract her, pleased to see the great black rain clouds rolling rapidly towards us. 'Quick, help me check the tarpaulins are tight.' For the next few minutes we tightened ropes and made sure our stock was safely covered. The rain was falling heavily as we tied up for the night. We retreated to the cabin and dug into the hotpot that had been simmering for hours. I broke up a nice crusty loaf and gave Brigid half to dunk into her stew.

We had reached Golden Valley, a beautiful place, but it wasn't the scenery that gave the valley its name. The people who used to live here toiled long hours in mills. It was the water that created the wealth for the mill owners, the jobs for the poor. Once there were flour mills and saw mills all about, but mostly the trade was wool, lots of wool, and occasionally cotton and fine silks. It was here that small children worked with their mothers from dawn to dusk to make the fine garments that were often carried by barge to London.

I couldn't see much further than the banks, no matter how hard I looked. If time was playing tricks again and the mills were working, I didn't know. We could see no further than a yard or so from the barge. The rain fell in sheets. We shut the cabin hatch door, sat inside by the stove and gently steamed. I decided that for once I'd be quite happy to listen to Brigid's crazy yarns.

'I always thought Gog and Magog were the greatest

giants,' I said. 'My dad says they came from Plymouth. My great-aunt lives there but I've never been, there's never been time. It was my great-aunt who sent me the book about Albion and Hercules. I felt really sorry for Albion.'

'So you should! Albion was my uncle.'

I gaped at Brigid, wondering if I claimed the pope as a relative, and told her how important he was, she'd claim him too.

'Anyway, it wasn't Gog and Magog, it was Goemagot,' Brigid continued determinedly. 'There weren't two giants, only one: Goemagot. Goemagot was brought to Troia Nova – London to you – by Brut after the battle that killed Albion. The one that wiped out all but the few giants tucked away in Cornwall.'

'So why was Goemagot allowed to live?'

'Brut had plans for him.'

I licked my lips and split another loaf. The stew was miraculous, or maybe it was the effects of the work and the rain. I wondered whether the people of yesterday also felt that a full stomach was more valuable than silks or gold.

'Goemagot was taken to London. Brut had him guard the door of his palace. As far as Brut was concerned, Goemagot was now a willing slave and doing his best to please.'

I swirled my stew rapidly round the pot. Why did I feel so angry? How did I know that the last thing Goemagot wanted to do was please?

'One day,' Brigid continued between mouthfuls, 'Goemagot sneaked the Cornish giants into the camp while there was a festival to the goddess Diana in progress. Brut and Corineus and their armies were very merry after drinking vast flagons of wine.'

Brigid was watching me, watching me very carefully. I shuffled uneasily, wondering what it was she hoped I would do or say. 'And were they victorious?'

'No,' Brigid said, looking disappointed. 'As you found out when you read your book, giants have great strength but very little brain. All the giants except Goemagot were killed.'

'So why was he kept alive a second time?' I asked, trying desperately to control the butterflies that were beginning to dance in the depths of my stomach. I felt somehow I was drawing too close, too close to something I was not yet ready to see.

'Ah, this is where you come in!' Brigid exclaimed, her expression one of sheer triumph. 'Not the *now* you, but the you that is Guendoloen. The giant Goemagot was kept alive because your father, Corineus, loved to wrestle with giants.'

'*My father was Corineus*?' I gasped. 'How can my father be Corineus? How can I be that ancient? My father is Corrie, boring old boatman Corrie.'

'You're not listening, Guen! You were reborn. Everyone originates from somewhere. My line began with Nodens and Coventina, but because I was *never* born, things for me were different. I cannot live for long on the earth, not in a form like you, so my beginning is in a way my end. Your line began with Corineus, and has gone on and on, generation after generation, rebirth after rebirth. The thing is, will it end with you? Will you always be Guendoloen, slave to Brigantia and the sunwheel? Of course you will.'

I dragged our pot from the stove and scooped about for the last lumps of meat that lurked at the bottom. All the time I was fishing I could feel Brigid's eyes boring into me. Suddenly I wasn't hungry. The butterflies had turned to great howling beasts. I didn't want even to consider reincarnation, the idea was too deep. I looked for safer ground.

'So did the giant Goemagot and Corineus fight?' I asked, not liking to admit the dark thought that if Corineus really was my father, I'd like him to win even though Goemagot was obviously the hero.

'Goemagot did well at first. He reached out and grabbed Corineus. In that one grab he managed to break three of your father's ribs, two on the right side and one on the left. Imagine hands big enough to do that, Guendoloen. To crush a man's ribs with just one squeeze.'

'What happened?' I asked even though I had no need. I *saw* an earthy arena hastily scratched out for the fight. I *watched* an excited audience leaping and screaming encouragement as bets were placed and wild wagers made. I heard eager voices egging Corineus, my father, on and on. I *knew* Corineus as a proud warrior who, if he won, was assured that his army would follow him willingly to the ends of the earth. I reeled in shock as my father's ribs cracked in that first assault. I felt his horror at the thought of defeat, his knowledge that one of them must die, his determination it wouldn't be him. My heart started beating faster and louder. I was smelling, even tasting, fear, sweat and pride, all tangled up together, as an unarmed man, my father faced a hulking great giant in a dusty earth arena long, long ago.

My father had helped Brut conquer Albion, the greatest giant of all, and now Goemagot had all but smashed his lungs in his very first move.

'Corineus was a proud man,' I told Brigid. 'He couldn't fail, he couldn't lose face. It wasn't his nature. Corineus gained strength from his anger, an inhuman strength. He raised up Goemagot, threw him over his shoulders as if he was light as a feather, and ran as fast as he could to the nearest cliff . . .'

I saw my father running to the edge, his body running with sweat, his heart full of black anger and injured pride at being so badly hurt, his ribs paining him dreadfully with every move, adrenalin driving him on and on and on. I watched Corineus hurl Goemagot right over the cliff. I saw Goemagot's body tumbling down over the rocks, splitting open as it bounced about like a spinning stone. His blood was everywhere. The rocks were washed red with it . . .

'I saw it!' I admitted shakily. 'I was there. No, I imagined it.'

'Imagination, my foot!' Brigid said, her voice too cool and too calm. 'You encouraged him, you cheered him on! It was such a waste. The place is still called Goemagot's Leap. The results of some deeds last for ever.'

'I've never been there.' I felt empty and not, as I expected, relieved to have reached the end of one of Brigid's strange tales.

'You can learn *nothing* without me!' Brigid grasped my hand and sounded strangely possessive. 'How can you begin to understand when you've never left the river? I am here to teach you. I stand beside you, your master and your slave, to lead you back through the waters of time, to Habren's death and to my beginning.'

# 13 Brigantia

'That boat of yours swims well when no one steers!' a passing bargee shouted as we ran parallel.

I looked at him oddly. The same way he looked at me. By now our boats had separated, for we were moving up as he was passing down.

'Brigid steers,' I called after him and he waved cheerfully, but he still looked puzzled. 'I wonder why he didn't see you,' I said to Brigid.

'He looks only forwards,' Brigid said quickly. 'His eyes are probably jammed full of coal dust too.'

I giggled but I felt I had to be fair. 'The old man was very grubby, Brigid, but it's hard to keep clean when you shift coal for a living. The dust gets everywhere no matter how careful you are, and water has to be moved bucket by precious bucket. I'm lucky. *Brigantia* is so beautiful, and so unusual too. Did you know almost all narrow-boats have roses or castles as decorations but I have water irises and golden king cup. I have elegant swans and leaping fish, all the things you find in a river.'

'She's a boat apart,' Brigid agreed.

The night was quickly closing in so we decided to tie up at the next lay-by. I had had the usual hot stew simmering away on the stove, and now the sun had set we both realised we were ravenous. I pulled down the cupboard door that also served as a table, dragged plates from the shelf, and dipped into the pot, all from my place just inside of the door.

I was looking forward to reaching Brimscombe. George had told me about the great cradle that weighed the boats so that the correct levy was charged. The boats were actually floated on to the weighing bridge, which was then carefully lifted.

'Let's stop,' I pleaded. 'You might even be able to buy a new tunic. Everything round here seems to be getting more and more old-fashioned.'

'We don't stop! This tunic's fine. It will last me as long as I need it.'

I handed her a plate of stew. I knew my face was sulky.

'Your boat paintings are so beautiful,' Brigid said to appease. She traced her fingers round the leaves of the giant water lily leaf that adorned the wall behind our small book shelf. 'Why do you think this picture was never finished?'

'I don't know,' I replied, knowing she'd won. 'We always

thought it looked incomplete, that's why Dad put up the shelf. The space sort of dares you. We thought about finding an artist to fill it in but somehow we never have, somehow the very idea seemed like an intrusion.'

'A goddess should be there,' Brigid said, still fingering the huge green leaves. 'Someone like my mother, Coventina, the triple goddess of springs.' She gave me a funny look. 'Someone like that.'

For a moment I felt uneasy. 'Is a triple goddess like a triple monster?' I asked to distract her. I thought of my picture of Hercules and Geryon.

'Don't be ridiculous!' Brigid snorted. A triple goddess is to be revered, possessing three very powerful aspects. Coventina is one, Brigantia is another, that space could be for her. The greatest goddesses have always borne three faces. The faces are all different and at the same time all the same. It's quite simple.'

'Is it?'

'Of course it is,' Brigid insisted, her eyes going that cool icy green that spelled danger if you argued too much.

'Well, I suppose we need a water goddess or three,' I said hurriedly. 'The rivers do run low. We've had far too many long hot summers.'

'Yes, there's been too much destruction of the beautiful and too much careless waste of the earth's great gifts.'

I nodded, for once I felt at one with her.

'It's horrid not even being properly born. It must be nice

knowing who you are and why you are. Sometimes I envy the entity who is Gwen.'

'Perhaps I don't care who or why,' I said, sounding a bit defiant. 'Perhaps I'm just happy to live in the moment called now.'

'Then you're not as daft I thought, little Guen!'

I couldn't think of anything sensible to say, so I just carried on tucking into my meal. Brigid copied, but she still looked sad and lonely, as if she felt incomplete, as if she had never really belonged.

'I've often wondered who decorated this boat,' I said, more to stop the melancholy silence than in expectation of an answer.

'The gap was left deliberately,' Brigid told me firmly. 'Be sure that whoever painted it was under Noden's command. He wanted this narrow-boat to remind him of his greatest love, to remind him of his greatest rage. The artist somehow knew that because of Nodens, Coventina lost control of rivers and springs, even her named ones. He knew that until this time loop is complete, the land will have no living heart.'

I looked out across the cut. We were approaching Beales Lock and Bridge. The water moved slowly despite the recent rain. The evening sun shone harshly through the autumn leaves, splashing the embankments with great pools of vibrant colour.

'It looks all right to me,' I said, watching a kingfisher dart across the quiet cut. Its feathers, struck by the harsh sun, emitted flashes of brilliant green and blue.

'The summers are too dry. When the rains come they are too wet,' Brigid insisted. 'Things haven't been right for years.'

'It's just a blip in time,' I told Brigid. 'My dad says it's due to solar flares. The weather changes when they get extra active and leap out from the sun. It happens every eleven years or so.'

'Quite true,' Brigid said, and I was stunned by her simple agreement. I smiled, but far too soon.

'And why does the spirit of the sunwheel keep feeling she has to flare?'

I couldn't answer. It would not have been wise to answer even if I could. Brigid still had that look in her eye.

'The flames spiral because the sunwheel spins but cannot properly turn. Slowly she cools, slowly she dies,' she said.

'The sun is just a great chunk of fire,' I braved, scooping out the remains of our meal and feeding them to Den. 'And the earth is just a great chunk of mud.'

'Yes,' Brigid agreed, smiling a mite too sweetly, 'but the rivers, the rivers are the very essence of life. Without them there is nothing.'

I gave up. 'You look tired,' I told Brigid gently, and to my surprise she nodded agreement.

'This journey is taking so long. I have been waiting for it for ever and now I am here, I too don't really know what lies ahead. I only know we have to find Habren, and you and I have to heal the rifts of time that tear us apart.'

'What rifts? What rifts can there be when we barely know one another?'

'Not you and me,' Brigid reminded me. 'The me that was never born and the you that is Guendoloen.'

'Ah, Guendoloen!' I muttered, but Brigid, worn out from the work of the day, didn't rise to my bait. She slept sprawled across her small bunk and still she managed to look beautiful.

The cabin felt confining. I wasn't used to having strangers so close for so long. I closed the door quietly and left to sit in my favourite place, looking forward from the roof of the cabin. Den joined me, I sat holding him close and we were lulled back into tranquillity, calmed by both the gentle rocking of *Brigantia* and the dancing lights that flickered gracefully on the waters of the moonlit cut. My world began to look as it always did.

I stroked Den's silky ears and in return he licked my knee. There was something odd about the way Brigid treated Den. Sometimes she looked at him lovingly, sadly, other times she seemed to hate the very air he breathed. I gave him a cuddle, partly to reassure *me*. Den had been my constant companion for as long as I could remember, but more and more often now Brigid seemed more important to him than me. I watched the mist drift gently over the sleepy waters. I heard an owl hoot, the moo of a cow in a field nearby and was calmed.

Brigid's world was still strange to me. Her mind was full of ancient gods condemned to sleep fitfully under river and sea. Now their ghosts were rising, haunting me too. No matter how hard I tried to lock them away, peace would not come. I realised I was beginning to *need* her strange stories, and even worse, *I was beginning to feel her stories were mine*.

# 14 The sea god is angry

'It's not your fault that Locrinus was a two-timing toad!' Brigid told me smugly the following morning as we carted a pile of boxes across the towpath and up the steep little path that led to the post office *cum* pub *cum* country store in Bowbridge.

'Who's Locrinus?' I panted.

'Locrinus was your husband, Guendoloen. Can't you even remember the most important man in your life?'

'You're being stupid! I've not even had a boyfriend,' I retorted as I realised I was handing my invoice over to Mrs

Maple, who I knew quite well. Unusually, she was wearing a fringed shawl, a long black dress and had little old-fashioned glasses perched on her nose. I stared at her in amazement. 'What are you doing here?'

'How dare you be so rude! I work here. I own this shop. What are *you* doing here?'

I shut up and concentrated on looking sheepish. I didn't have a repeatable answer. I sensed Brigid was smothering hoots of laughter. I daren't look at her. I daren't do anything.

'I don't know what things are coming to these days,' Mrs Maple said, giving me another funny look too. 'Fancy being interested in young men at your age! It's just not proper!'

I gaped at her. This wasn't the Mrs Maple I knew, the one who kept making sure I bumped into her tall, good-looking sons.

'I don't go out with boys. I never have done,' I said, glaring at Brigid.

Mrs Maple peered at me over her pince-nez. 'Haven't you, dear?' she mumbled. 'Sorry, I must have misheard.' She carefully gathered up the hem of her long black skirts and stepped delicately over her sleeping cat so she could reach her till.

I stood silently as Mrs Maple inspected her paperwork, riffled in the old tin box she'd had in her family for years, and handed over the money, smiling as she always did once a transaction was completed to her satisfaction.

'That was odd, her being there,' I said as we headed back to *Brigantia*.

'Not really,' Brigid said. 'People move about all the time, but she's a screwy character, isn't she?' and she held up the hem of her tunic and minced until we were both hooting with laughter.

After that the day seemed normal enough though. Mrs Maple had always had a certain timeless quality about her, but time travel still confused me. It was odd seeing so many people with horses or mules. The cottages were in small clusters, the villages set widely apart. Plumes of grey smoke rose up from grubby chimneys; even the lighting was different, more yellow than blue.

We journeyed on. By sunset we were shattered. Brigid's beautiful face looked more weary than I had ever seen it before. I felt guilty. She wasn't used to the work. I made a real effort to be nice.

'So, who's Locrinus then? What makes you think that I married him?'

Brigid handed me my share of the huge fruit pie we'd bought from Mrs Maple.

'Your father Corineus was King Brut's right hand man. You were married to King Brut's son, Locrinus the two-timing toad, though he didn't have much choice really because his affair was decreed by my grandfather. I'll tell you all about Locrinus later. I want to tell you about my grandfather today because his story comes first.'

'Hang on, then,' I said, finishing my pie and regretting my moment of niceness. Once more I sensed complexities I didn't want unravelled. I brushed away the pie crumbs and went outside, spending far more time than I needed carefully checking *Brigantia*'s ropes, desperately trying to find the strength of mind to tell her I wasn't interested. I failed miserably. 'This is the grandfather who's Manannan?'

'My grandfather takes many forms,' Brigid said, pleased to have centre stage once more. 'Manannan, Neptune, Poseidon. Each race chooses a different name, a different dressing, but the sea god is always the same.'

'*Of course!*'

'What are you smirking at?'

'I just wondered if you came from outer space.'

Brigid remained unruffled. 'No,' she said, 'I told you. I rose, like you, from the river.'

I didn't argue.

'I told you Albion was my uncle?'

I nodded, trying to keep a straight face while I imagined her nose expanding to the size of an isthmus. A nose so long and so wide that all the giants in her crazy brain could safely stomp across together.

'That was long ago. Giants were normal then. Albion was full of them.'

I took my drink and went out to settle myself on the cabin

roof, that way I could at least look out at the stars while I was regaled with nonsense. Brigid followed, smiling quietly. Den walked close by her side. When she thought I wasn't watching she gently patted his head.

'Are you listening?' Brigid demanded.

I shrugged non-committally as I slurped cocoa. I felt irritable and edgy, it seemed the safest response.

'Manannan, my grandfather, was commanded by the creator to control the waters of life. He did his best, but the task was too big . . .'

'I know, I know, you've told me!' I said, but Brigid ignored me.

'Manannan handed the day-to-day organisation of rivers to Nodens, so he could better control the sea. There are many more rivers than seas and they are often small and tangly, so, because Nodens had much less power than Manannan, he needed help. My grandfather knew well enough that Nodens was a womaniser, easily distracted, so he gave him the most beautiful river goddesses to help him, in the hope they would keep his attention close to the water.

'The goddess Brigantia, the one your boat's named after, took control of the rivers Briant and Brent. Her name means High One and, as you will discover, Guendoloen, she is properly named.

'The goddess Boannan, whose named river is the Boyne, cared for the rivers of Ireland. I'll tell you about her in a minute. There were many goddesses, those are just the best known. On top of the river goddesses there were goddesses like my mother Coventina, whose base is Carrawburgh near Hadrian's Wall, and Latis and Sulis. Between them, they controlled wells, pools and springs.'

'He loved them all?' I asked opening my eyes wide and raising my arms in mock horror. Den, startled by my sudden movement, growled.

'No,' Brigid laughed, 'not all of them, and you have to remember, things were different then. There were not enough souls to cover the earth so the gods were kept very busy.'

'People producers then, factory managers.'

Brigid ignored me. 'My father was a bit free with his loving, I admit, but that was how it was when the world began. Populations are controlled by nature. Too many people and births must be reduced, a suitable culture usually evolves. If it doesn't, then sooner or later a catastrophe occurs leaving too few homes for Otherworld souls. Then the birth rate rises again to compensate. That's how the wheel of life turns. It's always seeking equilibrium. It never quite gets there, so onwards it spins.'

'You're saying souls are recycled!'

'Isn't everything?'

'Not people!'

'Why not? At first, Nodens adored Brigantia, but she was so clever she scared him half to death. Nodens realised that

Brigantia could suck power into her possession like a hungry black hole. After Brigantia, he's rumoured to have had an affair with Boannan, but he only ever really loved Coventina. Once they met, he had eyes for no one else.

'Life seemed good. Bellies were full and hearts were happy. The gods were kept busy and the sunwheel spun as it should, but then came the first great battle . . .'

'I know! It was when Hercules . . .'

'Not that battle! That was in Gaul. I'm talking about Albion. The king and the country. The land of the gentle giants.'

'So what destroyed this paradise?'

'An invasion by Brut and your father Corineus. They marched in and took over the land, ravaging everything. Within months Albion was no more.'

'I keep telling you! Corineus was not my father!' I screeched, knowing he was but needing him to be Corrie. 'My father is a quiet man, more like your stupid giants than a soldier.'

'Corineus *was* and *is* your father. Like it or not, you are Guendoloen reborn.

'Brut and Corineus landed at Totnes with their huge armies and marched across Albion killing giants every step of the way. The sea god was angry. The battle was very bloody and not very fair. The giants rarely fought. They didn't have an eye for trouble and failed to recognise the danger of the spear.'

I nodded dumbly. I knew, I remembered, even Albion didn't fight back, not until the first giant died. It was such a hopeless battle.

'The giants were heavy,' Brigid continued relentlessly, 'they were slow and few in number. One by one they died.

'Manannan felt awful, he had done his best to stop it happening. He had caused the waves to swell to the size of mountains in a bid to capsize the marauders' boats and prevent them reaching shore but, although many drowned, too many survived. Manannan caused all the storm clouds to burst so the land was dark, wet and muddy, but the giants were easy to find. The invaders were light and quick on their feet, the giants easy to fell with twisted spear and sharpened sword.

'Goemagot was taken alive but only as sport, to be taunted and killed later, like a badger dug out for the dog. It was awful, Guen! The earth was awash with gore and it was impossible to tell where the rivers ended and the sea of blood began. Manannan had done his best but the good times were over. Brut and Corineus were victorious.

'A few frightened people survived, hidden in caves, forests and mountains. Those that fought were killed or beaten into submission. Once the giants were gone the Keltoi lost heart. They surrendered, and for a while even the gods were abandoned.

'Brut knew he owed victory to Corineus and his

followers, so he promised his son Locrinus to Corineus's daughter Guendoloen.'

'I know, that's me,' I said, just to save her from the effort.

'Brut and Corineus had taken Britain together. With your betrothal to Locrinus, the future line should have been secure. It was supposed to be a new beginning, a betrothal designed to bring back order.

'Manannan was furious. He wanted the giants avenged, so he turned his attention to the slave Estrildis, who was a Hun taken in battle en route to Britain.

'Manannan gave her the ability to move as gracefully as the ripples on a tranquil sea. He made her eyes shine brightly as the sun-kissed water. He made sure Locrinus would fall hopelessly in love with her.'

'Bit like Nodens and Coventina, then?'

'No, not at all! Locrinus had no choice. Manannan made your husband fall in love with Estrildis, so you, Guendoloen, would be mad with jealousy; so Locrinus would have to live with dishonour and guilt for at least every moment Brut lived. He wanted to watch the slow destruction of the friendship between Brut and Corineus, which was closer than that between brothers. What he didn't predict was the death of Habren.'

'Why did he want Gwendolen mad with jealousy?' I asked, feeling a rising surge of fear mixed up with anger and pain. I grabbed Brigid's arm and pleaded to know more.

'*What was the point of destroying me?*'

'Ah,' Brigid said looking strangely sad, 'tales of revenge run twisted as rivers.'

'And why, Brigid, are we *still* going backwards in time?'

'It's the only way to reach Lydney. We have had to choose the time we need to travel and the customers to provide our means.'

'There's more to it than that, Brigid!' I insisted, but Brigid was too tired to continue the story. 'Wait 'til we get to Framilode. Once we reach the Severn, time will *really* spin,' she said.

'How far back?' I demanded, refusing to let her pass to her bunk.

'To the time of the Keltoi, to the time of Habren, then more . . .'

'And I just have to do as I'm told?'

'I saved you, OK? So, yes, you do,' Brigid declared, her mood dulling with the fading sun.

'But my fall wasn't an accident!'

'How do you know?'

'I just do.'

'The outcome is the same. I saved you and we have to go to Lydney Sands with *Brigantia*.'

Brigid soon slept but I couldn't. I climbed down from the roof and restlessly patrolled the gunwales, checking our loads were secure, tugging and patting canvases reassuringly damp from the rising river mist. Everything *looked* normal but it wasn't. Gwendolen called ever more strongly from my inner soul, telling me to explain to Brigid that no more than justice had been done. Pain filled both my mind and Gwendolen's and, each day, the edges between us grew more blurred. I was sharing her anguish. I was feeling her yearning for resolution. Gwendolen was *not* the ogress Brigid believed her to be. She was a woman, and hurting, and I held faith with her, believing that only when Habren was raised could the true healing begin.

I felt out of control, I was being sucked into a vortex of a past still largely unknown to me. I was teetering on the edge of black time, hating the strange, the unfamiliar. I was becoming more and more scared.

I cried out in anguish and Den ran to me, licking, snuffling, comforting. I gathered him up and held him tight. I breathed in the warm reassuring scent of his fur. I tried to fight. I tried to step back from the abyss. 'I am simply Gwen!' I shouted to the river that led me ever on. 'I am simply Gwen.' Den growled softly, as if warning me I had no choice. I *had* to step forwards to meet my destiny.

# 15 Guendoloen and Estrildis

As soon as we stopped work for the day, Brigid started: 'Estrildis the beautiful slave, the captive Hun made even more lovely by Manannan . . .'

'I don't care how beautiful Estrildis was! I don't want to know! I don't want to know any of this!' I turned petulantly away and watched the distant outskirts of Stroud merge into the twilight. Its wool mills were still busy despite the failing light. I could hear the huge wheels groaning as they turned. There'd been a spillage while we passed. The waters of the cut had puddled with bright red dye. *Brigantia* and I had passed through reluctantly, but Brigid was right, the dye did no damage.

'There was poor Locrinus,' Brigid continued doggedly,

'betrothed against his will, a victim of politics, doomed to wed boring old Guendoloen . . .'

'Gwendolen was not boring!'

'How do you know? If you're not Guendoloen reborn then how do you know *anything*?'

My anger rose uncontrolled, like molten lava sealed under pressure for aeons too long. 'Estrildis was a man-stealing bitch! I loved Locrinus from the first moment I saw him. Do you have a clue what love is, Brigid of the fairy-brain? Love is consuming, it's not easily switched on and off. I was thrilled when our families arranged the joining. Locrinus was pleased too.' I grabbed Brigid's hand and pulled her face towards me. 'I know Locrinus didn't love me like I loved him, but he was pleased. Pleased was normal in those days. It was a *good* start.'

'He was just obeying his father,' Brigid said, shaking me off. 'King Brut said he had to be nice to you because peace depended on it.'

'He wasn't!'

'He was. Listen, Guendoloen! Estrildis was the victim right from the start. Manannan chose her to divide your families, to create a pain far crueller than the sword. Locrinus could have said no, he could have turned away from temptation. He wasn't *forced* to take her.'

'Estrildis was a scheming little whore! She wanted money and status. She wanted to escape slavery. There was no more to her than that. Any male would have done, any man at all, but the cow had to choose mine. She had to steal Locrinus.'

Brigid sighed, she clutched her hands round her knees and gazed out across the water. For a moment we fell silent as we watched the mill workers walk home along the towpath. One man held a lantern above his head, a straggling group of men and women followed behind chatting quietly, the younger children were lagging, too exhausted to skip or play. It was amazing no one fell into the cut and drowned. 'We're going back to those days,' I whispered to Brigid.

'Yes.'

'No, what I mean is, most people in my time are expected to work very long hours for very low pay.'

'Poor Estrildis didn't get *any* pay,' Brigid continued when the mill workers had passed. 'She was tall, strong and blonde, she was clever and lovely to look at, but the important thing is she was sad and extremely lonely. The *last* thing she wanted to do was mate with the man who had dragged her screaming from her home as a spoil of war.'

'Estrildis was a schemer, a walking man-trap!' I snarled, so angry that I didn't absorb the fact Brigid held a clenched fist in the air and was sporting a look of sheer triumph.

'Poor Estrildis was a captive, a slave. Now she became a prisoner of a different kind. She was contained in a small house a day's horse ride from Troia Nova in an effort to stop Corineus and Brut hearing of the liaison. She was kept well away from the city and all her slave friends. She was guarded every minute, night and day.'

'She deserved to be locked up, she was a trollop!' I was screaming now, out of my mind with fury.

'She was dressed well and better fed but she became even more lonely than before. She was kept hidden for seven years. Seven years, Guendoloen! And all because of a stupid promise to your father. Locrinus loved her madly, but she didn't love him. She hated the very air he breathed. Locrinus had killed her father and brothers in one of his long wars; her mother now spent all day sewing clothes for soldiers; her sister was used as a whore.'

'As was Estrildis!' I yelled. 'What else was a female slave but a strumpet?'

'Estrildis went to him a virgin, that was part of her appeal. Estrildis's guards had been instructed by Manannan even before the invasion. He'd forecast the storm and promised them safe passage if she was dedicated to his command. He made sure she was kept as one of life's pawns. He had known she would have a greater purpose than serving the army.'

'A greater purpose? Is a greater purpose destroying the heir's family? Is a greater purpose causing the breaking of the word between two great warriors, between Brut and Corineus, king and right hand? Estrildis had no purpose, Brigid. She just wanted life's comforts and, to her, Locrinus was the key. She used him, she stole him! She took what was mine.'

'Estrildis had a great purpose,' Brigid said softly. 'Without Estrildis there would be no Habren.'

'Without Habren we could all sleep easily in our beds,' I retorted, moving so far away from Brigid I nearly fell off the cabin roof.

'Without Habren,' Brigid said, grabbing me and pushing me back into place, 'Albion would have had no revenge and justice would not have moved full circle. You liked the giants, you said so.'

'There was no *need* for revenge! The giants were doomed anyway. They were all men so they couldn't breed true.'

I turned my head and gazed out across the black water. Somewhere an owl hooted. I imagined him standing triumphant with a mouse in his claw. That's what I felt like, a dying, struggling mouse.

Brigid was relentless, she ignored my tears. 'There was poor Estrildis, a prisoner. True she was given a nice little house, but there she was, tied to her cook pot, not allowed to even walk with her guards in the cool night air. She was alone so much her mind numbed and it was almost a relief when Locrinus arrived at the end of a day, hungry and demanding favours.'

I found myself hunching up, as if that would protect me. Brigid grabbed my chin and forced me to look into her eyes. 'Estrildis was so sad. She wanted to escape, she wanted to go home.'

'That's not my fault!'

'Yes, it is. If you'd have set him free to follow his heart, he could have taken her to Troia Nova, treated her like a lady wife. Then she might have gone to him willingly, she might have been happy . . .'

'She might have got what she wanted, you mean!'

'Would you have been happy being kept as a slave? Well, would you?'

'If Locrinus loved her so much, why didn't he see that she loathed him? Why didn't he set her free? No, he couldn't do that. He couldn't see hate because there wasn't any. Locrinus saw lust, and to a weak man lust and love can sometimes seem much the same. Your grandfather, Manannan, didn't need to blind him, Estrildis did that! Estrildis was out to steal a kingdom, my son's kingdom.'

'You didn't love him,' Brigid said calmly. 'You couldn't have. If you loved him so much then why were you lingering in Plymouth when Troia Nova was the heart of things?'

'Locrinus said he needed a haven to come home to and that Troia Nova, as capital, was vulnerable to attack, so he wished to keep me safe. He told me he loved me, and I was foolish for I believed him. Loving blindly was my sin too, Brigid.'

'Locrinus wanted to break off the betrothal. He wanted to so much that he went to Corineus in secret, offering him more wealth than he could ever have accumulated fighting giants. Then he went to Brut, offering to raise a huge army for his next campaign, anything to get away. Both men refused.'

'They had to,' I whispered. 'Between Brut and Corineus a word was a life bond. Whatever else, they were men of honour.'

'They destroyed Albion.'

'It was an invasion, Brigid! In the time of the Keltoi, raids like that happened all the time.'

'Locrinus wanted to break his bond . . .'

'But he didn't, well not until Estrildis had eaten away his soul. Anyway, if you are right and Locrinus really loved Estrildis, he could have taken Estrildis abroad. He could have lived peacefully enough in some silly little love nest. He could even have taken the Hun back to her home.'

'He was the king's son, not free to do as he pleased.'

'He was free to neglect me, Brigid! He was free to break *my* heart.'

I saw the busy encampments of Troia Nova. I saw Corineus and Brut huddled together, laughing and drinking, dogs and spearmen all around them, planning their next battle. I watched the duty men checking their boundaries, armed with flaming torch and spear. Out in the darkness I felt the presence of gathering giants.

I *was* Guendoloen. Her sorrow rose up in me in a black mass of despair. I felt her consuming love for Locrinus and

Maddan, her son. I experienced her anger and her shame, but mostly I knew her heartbreak and desperation for justice.

'Picture me, Brigid, lonely, eagerly waiting for Locrinus day after day. And what was he doing? Not helping Brut, oh no, he was flaunting his bit on the side. Everyone knew, everyone but me. For ages I believed his lies, believed only his duties kept him away. It never crossed my mind that *I* was his duty, his obligation and, even worse, he'd never ever cared.'

'You didn't have it so bad,' Brigid said softly. 'You could walk along the cliffs, you could gaze across the sea, you had slaves to pamper every wish, every whim. Imagine Estrildis, all alone in a strange country with nobody to trust, no one to confide in. Imagine being alone and pregnant. Imagine being kept for seven years behind closed doors.'

'Seven years was never enough! Seven years was nothing compared with what happened to me. My father had just died when I discovered the truth. My father Corineus, who had given me nothing but love, who had betrothed me to Locrinus believing him honourable, believing our children would rule the kingdom. The discovery that Locrinus was a liar and a cheat killed him, I know it did.

'I had to stand with Locrinus by my side while they lowered my father into his burial pit. I had to stand calm while they laid beside him the things he would need on his journey to the Otherworld. His most trusted sword and spear to keep him safe, a flagon of mead and a silver cup to drink from, even one of his slaves, Odra, who loved him so much she decided to give up her own life so she could continue to serve him. I longed to give him my heart too, feel the release of the sword and go with him to the Otherworld, but I had to stay. I had to stay because of Maddan.

'I went home devastated and Locrinus came with me for the very last time. What did he do? Did he give me comfort? Did he let my tears dry on his chest as any proper husband should? No! He said that now Corineus was dead he was going to live openly with Estrildis. He said his father didn't care any more, but I knew King Brut, like me, was worn out with grief. When Corineus died, his ally and closest friend, so in a way did Brut. Brut was now so vulnerable he was *coerced* into letting Locrinus live with Estrildis, but he still insisted she wasn't made queen.

' "It doesn't matter!" Locrinus shouted at me. "He can't live long, not without Corineus to support him. Soon I'll do just as I please!" '

'I was *destroyed*. My small son Maddan heard Locrinus shouting at me, heard him mocking, screaming, full of derision. He saw him raise his fists to me and whimpered in fear. Even that was not enough, Locrinus turned on our child. He shook Maddan. "You're a weakling! I don't need you! I have another child, Habren, a beautiful girl with the heart of a lion." Imagine that, Brigid! Imagine your *father* telling you he *hates* you!'

I was weeping, trembling. Brigid pulled me close and wrapped her arms round me, though she said nothing and gave me no warmth.

'I was angry. I was *so* angry. At the very least it was my legitimate son who should be king, not the progeny of Estrildis.

'I couldn't let it happen, Brigid. The people never honour a slave's child. They wouldn't *willingly* follow Habren's edicts or give up their men for glory in the Otherworld. The people needed Maddan, born from the marriage commanded by Brut and Corineus. So when I heard of the unhappiness, when I learned of the increasing unrest, I knew I had to do something, not for me but for the people, for the country, for peace and for Maddan.'

# 16 Time for battle

'For over two long years neither Maddan nor I saw Locrinus. Maddan eventually gave up asking what he'd done that was so bad his father wouldn't come. Sometimes I almost wished that Locrinus would take him from me, just so Maddan could be treated as a king's son. We were so lonely, it seemed like all our people had forgotten us.

'When King Brut died, Locrinus became king and commanded the bards and druids to read his augury. He called the people to a great king-feast. Even I went. I had to see. And when everyone's belly was full of succulent honey-sweet pork and their brains mellowed by flagons of rich elder wine, he made them watch as the chief druid slayed his finest bull, one that even Hercules would have admired.

'The bull was gigantic, its horns were coated in gold to impress the people, its coat was black and combed 'til it shone, then sprinkled liberally with gold dust. When the bull snorted and rushed round the ring of sated Keltoi they fell silent in fear. Only the chief druid dared approach him. He clasped the king's own spear with two hands raised and thrust it deep into the bull's heart.

'The bull died with honour, Brigid. It walked slowly round the ring gazing, as if in disbelief, at the people who had nurtured it for so long. There was not a word, not a whisper from the people. They watched the perfect ring of blood forming before them. They watched the giant bull's rich blood pumping out and running down its split heaving chest and between its forelegs, as it approached the king without even a stagger.

' "I wish Estrildis to be queen," Locrinus shouted at the bull. "Bow to my command."

'The bull, shaken by the sound, shivered as it suddenly came to a stand. "Bow low to me!" ordered Locrinus. "Acknowledge me as the people's king." The great bull was weakened and dying but still it would have raised its head and staggered on had the king's druids not prevented it. The druids were bowing respectfully as if in honour of its death.

' "Long live Locrinus!" shouted the guardsmen, trying to incite the crowd. "Long live Locrinus!" came the echo, but it was small and rose from the lips of those too scared to stay silent. The people couldn't see the thrust of small daggers rising into the great bull's belly to make sure he didn't move.

' "I said, bow low to me!" Locrinus commanded the bull as he stood, arms raised, before the unwilling crowd. The bull's eyes were glazing over. His was an *unseemly* death. I had this sudden fear, Brigid. I wondered how Brut died.

' "Long live King Locrinus!" the chief druid shouted, lifting his arms to king and crowd. "The augury is good, the gods have declared themselves happy. The heavens are triumphant, Locrinus is all powerful and Estrildis is his rightful queen."

'After that there was no real choice and, as expected, the people clapped and cheered. Locrinus pronounced us divorced, wounding me with words more painful than any spear. He proclaimed me faithless, he claimed Maddan was not his true son, even though the people only had to look to see. He abandoned me, his lawful wife, to take up with a Hun slave.

'I thought the people had accepted Estrildis as queen because Brut had not denied her publicly, because the bull had seemed to give its blessing. But the people were not happy, their unease grew greater every day. They didn't know what to do. Their farms were thriving, their cattle were fat, their hens fertile, their barns soon to be stocked with grain. It was approaching Lugnasad, the time of the harvest, so they had no wish for war and, anyway, the augury had been written in blood. The bull had died with his honourable head laid sub-missively at the king's feet, but the people were still uneasy.

'Ignored by his father and by his people because they feared the wrath of the new king, my son Maddan still walked among them with his head held high. He didn't let them know how much they were slowly eroding his soul, grinding him into nothingness. I have never felt so desperate but, like him, I walked proudly and, like him, I died inside.

'Estrildis was queen and so Habren was treated like a princess. Nobody wanted to end up as the next sacrifice when the gods withdrew their favours. But gradually the Keltoi noticed change. "The gods are angry!" they whispered to one another. "They send the storm before the harvest. Our crops are wiped out. Our hens, sheep and chickens drowned."

'If Locrinus had kept Estrildis hidden, as he did before my father died, then only I would have suffered. Maddan could have kept his place as the rightful heir, and the gods and the people would have been happy.

'Soon the whispers became openly spoken words.

' "Estrildis might have been named queen by Locrinus, but Guendoloen is our *rightful* queen."

' "Yes, we were tricked. The gods are angry, now our animals die."

' "Why did Brut die so suddenly? Locrinus is a king with brawn but no brain. It's obvious Brut was *murdered*."

' "King Brut died of loneliness," declared the druids, but

the people would not believe, and the druids too began to have doubts. It is their task to be the voice of the people. They are the teachers and the listeners, they are the ears and the soul of the Keltoi.

' "The people are unhappy," the druids told Locrinus, but he wouldn't listen and the druids were afraid to say too much. Even a druid can be sacrificed if the gods . . . or the king . . . commands.

'All this time Nodens and Taran were water and thunder incarnate. It rained and rained and rained. Locrinus cut down seven great oak trees. He had the druids hollow them out and stuff them with slaves, as offerings to the thunder god Taran. They were burned alive, slowly, screaming, and still it rained and still there was thunder. The gods were not interested in burning bodies. They wanted justice, for the people, for me, for Maddan, my son.

'Locrinus thought he was of the gods, but he was mortal. He forgot that without the goodwill of his people he could easily tumble into oblivion.'

I fell silent, exhausted. My heart was bursting with bitter tears. I took Brigid's hand needing the comfort of her presence. 'Brigid you know all this. For all my sins, I loved him.'

Brigid nodded. She took both my hands, warming them gently, soothing their trembles. 'It's your story,' she said gently. 'It's the tale only you can tell, and tell it you must, for only then can the ghosts of the past be laid to rest.' I leaned against her, oddly comforted.

'The people grew secretive,' I said, calmer now for being comforted. 'They sent messengers to Plymouth, they summoned the grandsons of the giants, crossbred with the Keltoi, but still tall. They told me they still wanted Maddan as king. Everyone knew that only then would pigs grow fat and the land flush green. "You must go to war," they said.

'At first I was suspicious. I thought that the giant men had been sent by Locrinus to taunt me. We conferred for days. They sent many men, many honourable men from all over the land. They came in the night, secretly, but they promised that if I would lead them, they would willingly die, for what is death but a passport to the Otherworld, and what is life, if there is no honour?'

'What indeed,' Brigid said softly, but she still gripped my hands. 'But the giants wanted revenge for the humiliating death of Goemagot too, and they wanted revenge for the death of my uncle Albion.'

'Of course they did,' I said, surprised to find myself agreeing. 'Goemagot especially. At least King Albion died in battle, was buried with honour and not splattered over the rocks to be picked at by fox and by crow. Albion could rise from the Otherworld to beget the line of King Arthur, to become a friend of Merlin. Goemagot still rests in the Otherworld. Who knows when he will have the strength to rise again?

'It wasn't only the grandsons of giants who wanted to fight. There were so many people wanting justice that our army grew bigger. Later, it was said that even the stones from Plymouth Hoe rose to defend the honour of the land, turning from granite to soldier. We fought with the blessing of the gods, for Albion and for Maddan.

'The journey was not easy but we were not frightened, for Manannan gave Brigantia a great shield and sword and sent her to march with us. Brigantia struck the earth with her sword and caused springs to gush from the ground when we were thirsty, she made them vanish the moment we passed. If we needed shelter then trees became forests or bright sun changed rapidly to fog. Brigantia had never forgotten being spurned by Nodens. She understood my need for revenge. We became closer than sisters.

'There were great hordes of us marching and yet nobody knew we were there. There were so many angry people yet, in the end, we only needed a few. As we marched my heart grew lighter. I didn't fear battle or death. I only wanted life with honour, for me and for Maddan.

'I knew Locrinus had always worshipped the goddess Diana who could change light, mountain and wood to any form if she had a mind to. I knew he thought of her as his divine protector, believing that when he went to war, Diana would hide him well.'

'She couldn't. Her power was pure mythology.'

'I know, but Locrinus believed. I put my faith in Brigantia.'

Brigid nodded agreement. 'Brigantia was always the clever one. She had fewer powers than Diana, but with water you can conquer the world.'

'Brigantia granted us a safe journey,' I continued. 'We rested a while, watching, waiting. We chose our moment well. We wanted justice, of course we did, but we wanted as little blood spilled as possible. That's why we chose the time when Locrinus was in Troia Nova at a feast held to honour Diana.

'We waited patiently while he made his offerings: fresh flowers, a fatted calf, the sweetest wine. We waited all through the feast, not filling our bellies, or losing our skills through tasting the wine.

'Such a feast it was, Brigid. There was boar, ripe and sweet, a boar that had been fed all its life on milk and porridge. There was a golden cow, fed only on heather, herbs and the sweetest meadow grass. There was a huge golden cauldron overflowing with honey-mead . . .

'We lurked in the shadows as they took their fill. We watched Locrinus stuff himself until his belly swelled. We watched him drink until his eyes were as glazed as those of his bloody bull. When his head was muzzy and his body weak, we went to war.'

'That was cheating!' Brigid exclaimed. 'Where is the honour in that?'

'It was not cheating. It was using his own weaknesses to

save the loss of too many lives. We could have just knifed him in the back. We could have just dragged him off like a dog. We could have slain him, and Estrildis, and Habren. We could have pulled the skin from their bones bit by bit, or stuffed him in a log to appease Taran. We did none of those things. We marched in and declared war.

'The battle was short but at least Locrinus had a chance to pick up his sword, at least I gave him death with glory, and that was far more than he deserved. Before it was over more than one man died because he couldn't predict the path of Locrinus's drunkenly flaying blade. Locrinus died on his feet, he died honourably. We could have dragged him back to Plymouth to plaster his blood on the blood of Goemagot, or we could have put him in a ring and thrust the knife to read the people an augury from his dying blood and spilt entrails.

'I was so elated when it was over, so thrilled that Maddan would rule. I imagined fields springing once more with wheat and sweet green grass. I wanted to honour the gods of water, water the giver and taker of life. I commanded that Estrildis and Habren be offered to the River Severn. It was no more than customary. I knew he would not want them killed, for with the death of Locrinus the giants were avenged.

'I wanted Estrildis subdued back into slavehood. I wanted her so scared for Habren that she would never think to rise up again. I wanted them both to know that they owed their lives to me, and to Nodens, the brother of Albion and river god of

117

England and Lydney Sands. "Throw them in the river!" I commanded. "Enslave them there. Let Nodens see their fear and know that both Brut and Locrinus are dead. Let Nodens feel avenged for the death of his brother Albion. Let Nodens keep them in his waters until their fight is all gone and they become willing slaves." I expected them to be subdued. I expected them to be scared witless. Honestly, Brigid, *I never expected them to drown.*

# 17 Deadly distraction

'Nodens and Coventina barely noticed the battle. They heard the shouting and the screaming, but it was as if it was another world, another time. Imagine being so much in love that nothing else matters,' Brigid said when we had moored up near Framilode the following evening.

'That's so blind as to be stupid. That's not love, that's obsession.'

'It was love. It was pure love and it made me. There I was, nicely growing in the soup that brings life and, suddenly, almost before I'd begun, it was over.'

'What happened?'

'What happened was you commanded Estrildis and Habren to be drowned in the River Severn, that's what happened . . .'

'Not drowned, *thrown*!'

'What *happened* was Nodens was too far away, and too inattentive to be properly summoned. The result was guilt and mayhem and madness.'

'That's not my fault. You can't blame that on me!'

'Nodens had never failed before, never. He couldn't handle the situation. The Severn was his named river, then his special responsibility. Habren and Estrildis called his name, pleading for life, but their desperate petitions were ignored. The river received a sacrifice that was not needed, not demanded. The people stood on the edge and watched them drown, and all because of you.'

'The people let them drown because they knew I had given them to Nodens. Nodens was god of the river. If *he* had wanted a sacrifice, then that was *his* will.'

'He didn't!' Brigid stormed. 'The last thing he wanted was a sacrifice, especially of an innocent child!'

'I didn't know that! The people didn't know that. As far as everyone was concerned Nodens had decided the death of Locrinus was not justice enough.'

'Your people could have saved them.'

'Yes, and what would have happened? What was the rule, Brigid? You know the truth. If the river demanded a sacrifice, it had to be made. If anyone tried to rescue a soul that the gods demanded, their soul would be taken in its place. Estrildis and Habren were disgraced, not worthy of such a sacrifice. As far as we were concerned, Nodens had demanded and Nodens had received.'

'Nodens was filled with shame,' Brigid confessed, her face full of unshed tears. I took her hand, she seemed not to notice. 'He had failed his father Manannan. In his distress he decided that Coventina was to blame. He stormed off to meet her. She went to him lovingly, he went to her angry. They met on the edge of the Thames.'

'But it wasn't *her* fault, Brigid. Why does a woman always get the blame?'

'I know both had abandoned their duties, but my father wasn't being logical. To him, at that moment, Coventina was a river siren, born only to lead him into temptation. He had to destroy her power, and in doing so he destroyed his.'

'How could he hurt Coventina? She was pregnant. You said Coventina was expecting you.'

'He didn't know that. She never had the chance to tell him. He grabbed her, there on the riverbank. He was the tumbling water of a land storm, he was the angriest of river bores. He was as mad as Taran and just as destructive. Nodens, my father Nodens, shook Coventina until her life blood and mine were spilled. As fast as the madness had begun it was over, but it was too late. I was blood on the riverbank, and my mother was waxy white in the Thames.'

'What happened then?' I whispered, clutching Brigid's trembling hand.

'Nodens was mad with grief. He couldn't let us go. He changed himself into a dog that would for ever guard the riverboats, looking for you, Guen, an innocent risen once more from the Otherworld, the key to finding Coventina. That's why you were found on the river's edge, that's why you never ever wanted to leave the water.' Brigid reached over and lifted my chin. Her green eyes seemed to gaze right into my soul. 'You are the future. You can open the lock that sets us free.'

I opened my mouth to speak but Brigid raised her free hand to silence me.

'The River Thames snatched Coventina and took her into its depths to keep her safe, but rumour says that every now and then she still escapes to the Severn. She still searches for Nodens in the hope that things can become as they were.'

'She's mad, absolutely mad, if she seeks the man that killed her. Would you do that? Would you?'

'She knew he didn't *mean* to destroy her. Even though she rests in the waters of the Otherworld, she somehow knows that Nodens has searched for her from that day on. He created pure white water lilies to dress the river in her memory. My life blood was scattered on the bank. I too was condemned to patrol the banks and endless towpaths, searching for you, searching for my mother, searching for Nodens the shape-changer, Nodens who is both my father and your dog. Guendoloen, believe me, I searched for you until my feet were shredded. Me, who never properly lived and never properly died. I called to the gods of river and sea for help and only Brigantia guided me, only Brigantia came. All this for you, Guendoloen. You are the beginning and the end. You were the cause of the destruction of us all, you are the one who can bring us back.'

'Your first life didn't end because of me,' I told Brigid for what seemed like the millionth time. 'Brigantia was the goddess in my heart. I cared not a jot whether Nodens loved Coventina. You dare to shout at me, you try and make me die of shame, when it was Nodens, your own father, who in his anger killed his chosen woman and his own unborn child? *How is he better than me? Tell me that!*'

Brigid said nothing but at last her tears fell. Feeling desperately sorry for her, I spoke softly. 'Estrildis and Habren should have ended up with no more than a public humiliation. The soldiers were laughing and jeering and Estrildis and Habren must have been very frightened, but it was my victory, my warning to the people that my son would rule and there must be no more pretenders. Some of my men were waving banners proclaiming my victory over Locrinus. More were yelling out that Maddan was now king, but they did not hold Estrildis and Habren under the water. I gave no order to kill.'

'But they died!' Brigid said grimly. 'Because of you they died. Because of you, Nodens lost control.'

'No,' I said, smiling acidly at Brigid the unborn. 'They died because your father and mother were tumbling in the hay like lesser mortals when they should have been guarding the water! They could not resist the sins of the flesh and the cost was that the doors of the Otherworld opened unbidden.'

'It was an *accident*! You're from the killing line, Guen, not me. You killed Locrinus even though he was the father of your child!'

'I didn't kill him, I went to war. It was *necessary*!'

'I suppose you're going to tell me you didn't hate Estrildis either!'

'Of course not! I loathed her.' I stopped. It was no longer true. My anger had gone leaving only sadness for things that could have been. Brigid's face was ashen, her strength and determination gone leaving her as pale and trembling as the moonlit water. I felt only pity for us both, I realised we had both been victims. I tipped back my blankets and leaned towards her bunk. I grasped her shoulders and shook her gently back into the safe secure world of *Brigantia*'s cabin. 'I am not guilty,' I told her firmly. 'You are not guilty. Like Habren, we are not culpable. We have moved on.'

'We inherit the guilt,' Brigid whispered, her eyes still full of crystal bright tears. 'That's why we are here.'

'We inherit the ability to make amends too.'

'So even though you blame me, Guendoloen, you'll help me wake Habren?'

'I don't blame anybody, Brigid. It's just history, it just

happened. As long as we learned, as long as next time . . .'

'So you'll still help?'

'Of course,' I said, smiling as I reached out to flick Brigid's sunwheel. 'We've come so far, learned so much, and with the rising of Habren we are both cleansed. I wouldn't miss the chance of waking Habren for the whole wide world.'

Brigid smiled back, and her sunwheel began to glow.

# 18 Nodens reborn

High in the Severn where river meets sea, there are strange eddies and whirls everywhere. Sometimes I felt really scared, but we had an ebbtide so we made good time to Lydney Sands. *Brigantia* often seemed out of control, it was as if she too was eager to arrive. Brigid and Den were no help at all, they stood looking down river, waiting, anticipating.

As soon as Brigid was happy we'd arrived at the right spot, the spot where her sunwheel spun forwards and back as confused as the tides, I made haste to tie-up, but Brigid would have none of it. 'The boat must drift, find her own destination.'

'Can't we rest? Can't we have a really sticky bun, or fetch a huge ice-cream? Can't we *celebrate*?'

'There's not much time. It's the eve of the winter solstice.

We only just made it. Nodens will rise tonight.'

'Oh, yes, Nodens,' I said, yawning. The journey had been exhausting and I'd lost count of the locks we'd passed through, but I'd fulfilled my promise. I wanted to whoop and dance and enjoy feeling smug. I'd kept my part of the bargain, now I wanted to be free.

'We must believe.' Brigid tugged at my arms. She sounded quite desperate. 'Both of us.'

'I believe,' I replied, not caring what and too tired to argue. 'But I'll stay here by the tiller, just in case we need to allow another boat to pass.'

To my relief Brigid took my words at face value. She stood fore-end of *Brigantia*, staring restlessly out towards the sea.

The night became chilly, the stars twinkled crisply in the pitch black heavens. The winter fresh-air die-hards had long ago drifted home. The night fishermen passed us on their way to the open ocean. I expected *Brigantia* to drift seawards but she didn't. She sat where fresh water meets brine as solidly as if an anchor had been dropped to restrain her. The moon shone brightly.

I don't know why I kept watch, instinct I suppose, even though there was nothing to see, just distant lights on the bank and twinkling lights bobbing about on their way to the sea. We waited silently for hours but I felt no cold. The gentle movements of *Brigantia* lulled me. I stood in a world of my own, half watching Brigid, half lost in the comforting stillness.

Suddenly Brigid stood and stretched out her arms. 'We have come when the moon wears her fullest face. We have come. We are here, slayer and slain. We are here. We watch as the life-giving sun rises. We watch before the full-faced moon sleeps. We are here.'

She stood silently staring at the place where the river meets sea. She looked like a goddess, standing there in her white linen tunic dusted with gold.

'Nodens be summoned!' she suddenly yelled, and I was so startled I leaped to attention and nearly fell over. 'I have kept the pledge demanded of me. For centuries I have searched the endless rivers. I have brought back Guendoloen as the sunwheel commands. We need you to help wake Coventina. We need you to help us wake Habren. I need to see you, Nodens, my father but, above all else, Habren, as promised, must rise.'

Brigid turned her face towards Den. He growled softly. I went to stroke him but he stalked away and stood alone at the fore-end of *Brigantia*. Brigid followed him, grabbing his head to force him to look her in the eye.

'Nodens the shape-changer, wake now, for we are rapidly running out of time. Nodens, Father, the punishment is over.' Brigid released the dog's head. He stood still, watching her as she continued to speak.

'Brigantia is about to restore all our fortunes. She says the demands of earth, sea and sky will be understood once more, that they will rest at the very heart of this new millennium. She says only then can the destructive forces of man be restrained. Nodens, after all my efforts, will you refuse to hear me?'

I looked at Den. He turned towards me as if saying goodbye. Suddenly he began to change, growing before my eyes. Slowly he raised himself on to his hindlegs, doubling then more than trebling in height. I was stunned into total silence as the giant dog became muzzy at the edges and his limbs slowly lengthened, his fur melting away to display strong tanned and healthy flesh. This time I felt brave, this time I reached out to touch. Nodens felt like solid man not fickle shadow.

Nodens looked round as if a bit confused and shook his head. He was not the least bit like Brigid. The water which had been so calm, tumbled back into the estuary as if angry at being woken, bubbling, roaring, sending mud, sand and pebbles tumbling in all directions. Bits of stone glittered like silver stars as they were lit by rising sun and sinking moon.

*Brigantia* began to rock violently. I grabbed the tiller but she didn't respond. The river was rising, boiling, seething. I was sure *Brigantia* would be torn apart or hurled into the bank or would drift desperately until the tide ebbed and we were taken down towards the distant sea. Brigid turned her back on her father's angry face, she stared over my head and up-stream.

'Spirit of Brigantia, give us the help we need. We are your handmaidens for, in truth, you are the strength of us all.'

Water and sea instantly calmed. 'Where does Brigantia come into all this?' I dared ask Brigid at last.

'Just for a moment Brigantia forgot us, that's why the tide raced so high. Remember, she too was loved by Nodens.' Brigid glared at her father, as if daring him to lie. 'Brigantia was his first and his favourite river goddess, that is, until he saw her strengths and in them his own weakness.'

'I thought Coventina was his favourite,' I said, not daring to look the great man in the eye as I spoke, especially when he shrugged and winked at me.

'She was. Brigantia held sway until Coventina, curious to know what she was missing, left her springs to meet him. Brigantia would have dumped him sooner or later anyway. She would, Father, you know that! If anyone has the power to move things, change things, use things to her advantage, it is Brigantia. It is the very spirit of Brigantia that pulls the life strings that bind Habren, Guendoloen and me.'

'Daughter, you *know* I want only Coventina,' Nodens said. 'Brigantia is, as always, free to do as she wishes.'

'Yes,' Brigid said, looking a bit smug, 'and she will.'

'Why didn't he say hello?' I asked and Brigid's face told me what I already knew. Nodens, the shape-changer, had always walked with us.

He wandered off to look out towards Lydney Sands.

'What's he doing now?' I asked, still thinking him rude to ignore his own daughter.

'He's remembering how Coventina died. How I died. He's wondering what form Brigantia will take in the new millennium. He's wondering why she let him lie so quiet all these years. He's no good at river control, not really, he wants out. He's not responsible.'

'I think it's funny, your father being a two-timing old toad like Locrinus,' I said, grinning widely.

'Neither of our families is perfect,' Brigid agreed, 'but we Keltoi gods are born to live with earth, sun and sea. We are the heart of the river, the pulse of the earth, the soul of the sky. If the people listen, then there is balance and the sunwheel spins more brightly. We listen to the wind that knows it blows too strongly because there are not enough trees, sending our precious earth up in great drifts to the sky. We hear the distress cries of felled trees. Our nostrils fill with the warning odours of polluted rivers, dying fish and unhatched birds.'

'The people were often scared, you said so yourself. Look at Taran. He demanded horrific sacrifices. The people were scared of you too. They didn't want to be sacrificed. It wasn't all wonderful, Brigid, you know that it wasn't!'

'It was better. Most of us did our very best to preserve the gift we were given. There were only a few bad gods like Taran, and he, like most of us, was led gently into evil. Before the new millennium is born, someone will deal with him. Taran grew to see power in numbers of bodies. He took what was not his to have. It will stop.'

'You could have stopped him sooner. You could have done something then.'

'Everything has a natural time, Guendoloen. Our ways can appear harsh, even to me. Our function was, and is, to give back what the earth, our earth, demands for life, the land and the river, the sky and the sea. Sometimes life demands the odd sacrifice, steals the odd body, but the gods don't ask for deliberate death, you knew that! You said yourself that Estrildis and Habren should never have died. Even Taran didn't ask. He took what was given.'

'But people died, screaming!'

'I died too . . . yes, it's true, Guen, I *should* have accepted earlier. But it's hard when it's personal and the result could be catastrophic. Everything is recycled but, for life to be replenished, the sunwheel *must* turn. I'm still here, I who was never even born. Long-dead people still exist, people as ordinary as the Mr Bristow and Mrs Maple you know so well. Surely you understand that now?'

'I understand a bit,' I admitted, 'but I still think you're a very odd crowd.'

'I know we're not perfect, but we're no different from you and we're doing our best.'

'We could learn from each other,' I said, wanting the lecture over.

'Sure we can, and we will.'

'So, about Brigantia?'

'Brigantia was filled with jealousy. . .'

'No,' I struggled to unravel the mists in my mind. 'Not about loving Nodens and being spurned . . .'

Brigid said nothing. I gave up and looked towards Nodens. He was still lost in a world of his own. He was softness and power all mixed up in one. I could see why the water goddesses fell for him. I was more than a bit moved myself. I had every sympathy with Brigantia.

'Brigantia was broken-hearted when Coventina stole Noden's cheating heart,' Brigid continued.

'So if she's angry with Nodens, why is she helping us?'

'Manannan made Nodens the master. With him skulking away in the form of a dog, we Keltoi gods slowly faded from memory. Our imprint on this earth was forgotten, the land was neglected, earth, sky and water ravaged. The sunwheel became sluggish and hard to turn. Manannan has now agreed that Nodens cannot cope, not even with help. He has decreed that in the new millennium Brigantia will be made all powerful so our voices can be heard again. Brigantia will restore the fortunes of our earth.'

Nodens shifted about like an embarrassed child. 'I could cope!' he roared. 'You judge me too harshly, daughter. I never meant to betray Brigantia. I never meant Estrildis or Habren to drown. I met Coventina and I was on fire. I loved your mother so

133

much that nothing else seemed to matter. Brigid, I wasn't useless. I just loved her too well, I still do. Is it a sin to love too much?'

'Yes,' Brigid retorted. 'You showed you lacked the strength of Brigantia, who has never forgotten she has a purpose.'

Nodens hung his head in shame before his daughter.

Brigid offered her father neither smile nor condemnation. If she had received gifts from her parents at conception, they were their strengths not their weaknesses. Brigid was proving to be a worthy servant of the new Brigantia.

'Here is the word of Brigantia, the greatest triple goddess of them all,' she told her father calmly. 'You may have Coventina, but she too must be warned that if she ever neglects her duties again, man will waste water, springs will run dry and neither of you will be forgiven. You are, of course, permitted to help her. Perhaps all will be well if you work as a team. Be warned, Nodens, this is your final chance. If you fail, death and rebirth will surely follow, in different places and at different times. You will lose Coventina for ever.'

I expected Nodens to tell his daughter she was right out of line, but he didn't. He looked humble and scared.

'Habren may rise,' Brigid continued, 'and, because she is the face of death reborn, we may all see that, at last, the sins of the past are forgiven and there is hope for the new millennium. I am the voice of the future, listen and all will be well.'

'Not easy. That is a hefty price.'

'The cost of love is power, soon to be rightfully transferred to Brigantia. We have a final chance to restore the earth to balance. With Brigantia ruling, the sunwheel has its best chance of spinning eternally.'

Nodens smiled, and his smile lit fires of red in the puffy clouds that had risen with the dawn. He rested his hand on his daughter's shoulder. 'Brigantia is the right choice,' he said softly, and I knew that he, like me, suspected that Brigid and Brigantia were one. 'The dawn of the new millennium is the time of Brigantia, her chance to make things well. I choose Coventina. I choose to release you.'

Brigid just nodded where I would have shrieked in delight. The drama, for the moment, seemed to be over.

'What about me? What about *my* dog?' I asked her. 'Do I have one? Is he dead?'

'If there was a dog, there is a dog. Death is nothing, just a rest before rebirth. Den's fine.'

'Will he go home soon? Will I? I don't want him dead.'

'Resting.'

'In the Otherworld, then? I want my dog!'

'Den has already returned,' Brigid said, taking my arm, 'and soon your family will welcome him back with open arms . . .'

'And where will I be?' I screamed.

'You will be with him,' Nodens said, giving Brigid a look I couldn't quite fathom. 'Where else would you be?'

'Stop worrying!' Brigid said, taking my arm. 'Everything

has a natural time. How often must I tell you? You really must learn to live in now.'

The waters of the River Severn stirred uneasily as she spoke. I was left with the wary feeling that Brigid's truths were sometimes as fickle as Noden's shifting sands.

# 19 The needfire

'Will Estrildis rise with Habren?' I asked as we made preparations for her emergence from the Otherworld.

I was pleased something was about to happen at last. Nodens and Brigid had been playing happy families for days, in between stalling all my attempts to leave.

'How come there is so much time now?' I asked petulantly, 'when before there was so little?'

'This is a waiting time,' Nodens said, his voice deep and rich. 'It is a time to assess, a time to grow, a time to prepare ourselves. We might look idle but Habren knows we are waiting, all of us. She will take strength from our resolution. She will know when to come.'

'And Estrildis?' I asked.

'Estrildis's task is over,' Brigid explained. 'She lived this life to give birth to Habren who was born and has died as decreed. One day soon, Estrildis will rise from the Otherworld and be rewarded for her efforts. Estrildis will be granted freedom, absolute freedom. Never again will she be anyone's slave.'

'What if she just wants to live her life once more with Habren?'

'She can't! Hers is the absolute sacrifice. Habren's death holds too great an importance. Estrildis will be happy though. She will never remember this lifetime's sorrows, and Habren, like you and me, must step out of her circle of time. She is chosen, one of us, and we are the voice of the new millennium.'

'Brigid, we are children, small cogs in big wheels, why should anyone ever listen to us?'

'Someone has to be listened to,' Nodens chipped in, 'and it's often the innocent voice of a child that drops the pebble that starts the ripple that builds into a flood of good intent.'

'We're so ordinary,' I said, meaning me rather than Brigid even though I didn't say.

'Believe me,' Brigid replied, 'we are not ordinary. Was it ordinary taking a boat through time? Was it ordinary turning winter to summer? Was it . . .'

'I still feel Estrildis should rise with Habren.'

'That's guilt talking!'

I wanted to argue that it was fairness, but I couldn't. Brigid was right, it was guilt, so I just nodded. She reached out and touched my hand.

'If death does not occur in the usual way it has some hidden purpose. Souls are not lost, neither are they wasted. They travel to the Otherworld to be reborn. Estrildis will forget Habren ever existed in her past, just as you forgot you were Guendoloen.'

'But what if someone makes her remember?' I asked, giving Brigid a long, significant look. 'What then?'

'She'll never remember more than shadows,' Nodens said firmly. 'The most that will happen is she'll be scared of water, or extra possessive over her future children. Estrildis will not suffer. Her reward is eternal contentment.'

'What's it like dying?' I asked, wondering if the Otherworld was like heaven, or hell.

'The soul just steps out of time. It is allowed to rest for as long as is needed. If a life has been hard the sleep may be long. Otherworld souls are given love and kindness, and when they are ready to face earthly chaos again, they return, reborn, a new baby, a new life.'

'So you think all babies are reborn?' I asked, not sure whether to mock or feel relief that I wasn't alone.

Brigid nodded. 'The Otherworld is big, but not that big. Everything has a natural cycle, it is eternal life in the very best way. We are forever growing, we can learn from past keys in our souls, we are one with the earth.'

'And when the planet cools and dies?' I asked, trying to catch her out.

'The planet collapses, it becomes a black hole. It sucks in matter and, eventually, is reborn as a new star. We sleep, then are summoned back from the Otherworld as needed, and the whole cycle is repeated.'

'Who's in charge next time – Brigantia?'

'If you mean in the new millennium, yes, for Brigantia is the water of life. It needs a creator however to give birth to a planet.'

'So even Brigantia is a cog?'

Brigid laughed. 'Of course Brigantia is a cog, but one in the fundamental mechanism!'

'Of course!' I replied, a mite sarcastically, but Brigid remained unflustered. 'Come, we have work to do. December is almost ended, a needfire must be built, Habren must rise. Who am I to question the creator's needs?'

'Where will Habren rise?' I asked, longing to meet her.

'Habren is more of the river than sea,' Brigid replied thoughtfully, 'so I guess we must travel inland, go back towards Framilode.'

'You *guess*!' I shrieked, clapping my hands in delight. 'Are you telling me that after all this knowing, you guess?'

Brigid chuckled, 'Well, maybe I don't guess, maybe it's more truthful to say I wait until the sunwheel commands.'

'I rather liked the guessing,' I told her as we travelled back.

The going was hard this time for we ran against the tide. Here and there it was a struggle to move forwards.

'Why wouldn't Nodens come?' I asked.

'He daren't be distracted, not for a moment. He's busy listening out for Taran. Since Samhain, all the old gods have been slowly waking. Taran, as you've guessed, was one of the first. This time Nodens mustn't fail, he must protect Habren. He must outwit Taran, who grows more dangerous by the moment. I'm scared, Guen. Taran's planning something bad. He's been quiet for far too long.'

'Did you know he would wake? Is everything planned?'

'Everything,' Brigid replied, and she had the decency to give me a sheepish grin.

'So where is choice?'

'Choice is Nodens neglecting the Severn, and look what happened then. Think about it, Guendoloen, how much of what we do is really choice?'

Words like commitment, common sense and obligation flashed through my mind. The more I looked for choice the less I found.

'Habren's body would have drifted downstream,' Brigid said, sounding remarkably cheerful as she interrupted my reverie. 'Well, not drift exactly, because if the bore was high it could have shifted her down miles, even out to sea. We have to find the place where she rested long enough for the gates of the Otherworld to swing open so she could be snatched to safety.'

I shuddered, guilt overwhelming me as I thought of Habren, much the same age as my son Maddan had been, becoming a limp body, victim of the whims of the waters of the River Severn.

'You're quiet,' Brigid said, linking her arm through mine. 'Problem?'

I shook my head. How could I explain the black emotions of the past that were rising up from the depths of my soul and threatening to drive me mad with grief?

'There is always hope,' Brigid said, and for once I accepted her mind-reading gifts with relief. 'If we remember the past and build for the future, there is always hope.'

I said nothing. A little bit of me was still longing to retreat into the innocent isolated Gwen of the past.

'Say something!'

'I feel like a chicken in a shell. I feel as if the shell is crumbling all round me and I am too frightened to hatch.'

'You're not frightened really,' Brigid said calmly. 'You're just not quite ready.'

We moved further and further up the Severn, mostly in silence. Brigid was concentrating on looking for Habren while I was steering and trying to work out who I really was and who I really wanted to be. I wasn't proud of being Guendoloen, but, unlike Gwen, she *lived* her life, she felt deeply, she knew who she was.

We reached a spot where the river narrowed and twisted.

The face of Brigid's sunwheel changed from plain to vibrant, it began to shimmer and spin. The three faces I'd seen before emerged and faded, the three faces of a goddess, strange yet familiar.

'We are here,' Brigid said, smiling. 'Tie up quickly. This is the place, and we have little time for soon it will be dark.'

We set off along the bank with bags of food, warm clothes and lanterns to light our way when needed. 'We will rest a while,' Brigid told me just as I was about to nag her to death, 'for soon we must build a needfire.'

'What's a needfire?'

'A fire we need to wake Habren.'

'Is that all?' I asked, feeling somehow disappointed in so short an answer.

'A needfire is used as a communicator between gods and people. Habren was born of the people and, like you, she has bridges she must cross. A needfire is usually built at festivals such as Beltane to plead for fresh green pastures, or at Samhain where the normal barriers are broken and Otherworld spirits can easily rise to walk the earth. You fell at Samhain, don't you remember? And that, of course, is when I rose. The needfire is an essential part of any transition, the very heart.'

Brigid and I felt close to each other now. In baring our souls we had tied ourselves together. Even when pleading to go home, I had known it would tear me apart to leave. 'Will

I like Habren?' I asked, wondering how things would change between us.

'Yes, don't worry. I bet you'll feel as if you've known her years.'

'Possibly. You've spoken of almost nothing else since the moment we met.'

Brigid laughed, and we spent the next hour chatting as we busily gathered wood, everything from small kindle to great logs. By the time we had finished we needed *Brigantia*'s nightlights to see.

'Do we light it now?' I asked, giving Brigid a lump of rather stale bread and a cup of rather tepid soup.

'When we've eaten. A needfire has to be attended properly. A feast is OK, honourable; a paltry snack is not suitable for such a great occasion. Better to fast by the needfire.'

I glanced up at the new moon, a faint silver curve in a very black sky. 'We could have done with a bit more light.'

'No, this is perfect, for when Habren rises she must be sheltered from all light.'

'Why?'

'The gates only open in darkness and bright light after so long in the dark is unbearable. Habren's eyes, like ours, need time to adjust. Would you have her frightened?'

'Won't she burn in the flames?'

'No.'

'Why?'

'You'll see!'

I gave up, collected our cups, switched off the lamps and carried them out of the way. Brigid handed me the sunwheel. 'You hold it over the fire and I'll do the talking.' Not much change there, I thought, but I said nothing as I raised the sunwheel over the unlit fire. I held it until my arms ached, gazing as instructed, right into its centre. I was about to give up when I saw flames where before I'd seen faces.

Brigid stepped forward in that same moment and lit the fire.

'New moon grant us our wish,' she intoned as she lit the catch-wood.

'Earth and river and sky gods hear us. Bring us Habren, risen, for without her the sunwheel cannot properly turn.'

Brigid alternated between looking at her growing flames and the crescent moon. I watched the sunwheel, spinning, turning. The flames I had seen in the centre became a face. The face became Brigid and then me, and finally a dark-haired girl I just knew would be Habren. The faces merged and were gone, I ended up unsure whether they had ever existed anywhere, except in my addled brain. Unnerved, I handed the sunwheel back to Brigid, who seemed to hesitate before accepting it.

The needfire flames burned brightly but only on one side. A cloud passed across the virgin moon, and in that moment of total blackness the flames leaped from one side of the pile of wood to the other. No messing, a straight swop from side to side. My mouth dropped open.

'Habren has crossed over,' Brigid whispered before I could open my mouth and spoil the mood. 'In a moment she will rise.'

The flames were swirling round, forming a small column. 'No one could rise and live in those,' I whispered back.

Brigid nodded and pointed. 'Nodens is in command, see?'

A huge cloud had swirled down from the sky and wrapped itself round the shaft of fire protecting it from earth and moon. There was no steam, no smoke, no sound, just thick black swirling mist.

'What now?'

'We wait,' Brigid said, her voice still quiet. 'We rest and wait. Nothing will happen until dawn.'

As the sun rose, the smog round the small misty column began to clear. Habren's form grew stronger by the moment as she warmed in the growing heat from the sun. She stood, small, her skin pale as if from years of sleeping, her hair dark and curly, her eyes earthy brown.

Brigid stepped forward to greet her. 'Habren, spirit of river and earth, welcome.'

Habren smiled and offered Brigid her almost translucent hands. 'You must be Brigid, for even in the dark your skin shimmers as if lit by the sun.' Brigid nodded. 'Yes, yes, but look who I have here! This is Guendoloen.'

Habren turned her gaze towards me. My heart felt heavy. I lifted my eyes expecting hatred, expecting to have to defend my actions all over again.

'I didn't want you to die!' I told her desperately. 'Neither you nor your mother. I only offered to Nodens the rights that were his.'

Habren nodded. 'I know that, Guendoloen, essence of river and moon.'

Essence of river and moon! I turned to Brigid, the Gwen that I seemed to be rapidly losing, suddenly back. 'What is this? Is she as crazy as you?' As the words burst out I felt foolish, for the person talking didn't seem a bit like me.

Brigid glanced uneasily at Habren and gave her a look that warned her to take care. 'She is not ready . . . not yet.'

'Time is running out and she has much to learn,' Habren said, her tone both quiet and determined.

'Not now!' Brigid pleaded. 'Not yet.'

'She must know that we are of the river of life,' Habren replied, as if I was deaf as well as stupid. She brushed the last ashes from the needfire from her plain brown tunic. 'Water does not run alone, it is influenced by earth and sun and moon. I am sensitive to the voice of the earth. Surely Guendoloen knows that I must be, having lain so close to its heart from the moment I was slain . . .'

'I'm sorry, Habren.'

'There's no need, you know there's no need,' Habren said,

turning her pale face towards me. 'I am Habren, I too am . . .'

'Hungry!' Brigid said quickly. 'I too am hungry. Let's go back to the boat and later, when we have rested and eaten, we can tell Guendoloen everything.'

I pretended not to care that they plotted against me. I knew Brigid, I knew when she lied. I was sure the very last thing they'd do was tell me *everything*.

# 20 Coventina

Nodens was waiting for us when we returned to Lydney Sands. I noticed his hair looked shiny black but here and there it grew white, as if touched by old age. Images of my dog, Den, suddenly flashed through my mind. I missed him. I desperately hoped that he was safe at home.

'It's the trouble with being a shape-changer,' Brigid whispered. 'They always look a bit like the animal form they take. You can only tell if you look carefully, but the white streaks are a bit of a giveaway, aren't they?'

'Den is safe?' I checked.

'He's perfectly safe. I promise.'

This time I knew Brigid spoke the truth. I smiled in relief.

'As you've guessed, Nodens has been with us from the start,' Brigid explained. 'That's why Den didn't bark when you fell, that's why he made no sound at all. Nodens had taken over, Nodens was in control, but Den is free now, more free than he's ever been.'

'Are you ready?' Nodens asked when he'd quite finished hugging Brigid and grinning like a Cheshire cat at Habren and me. 'We must cover the water with river flowers.' He spread his arms expansively over the sea.

'River flowers? In December?' I nudged Brigid. 'Come on, I can't wait to see this. If you can make the winter sun warm, you can do anything.'

'I can't make flowers bloom in a day, and even if I could, there wouldn't be nearly enough to cover Lydney Sands.'

Nodens grinned. 'You can't but I can.'

Brigid, Habren and I looked on as blue skies rapidly turned grey and the temperature dropped steadily. Habren seemed curious. Nodens and Brigid were acting all uncon-cerned. I was becoming goose-pimply. I couldn't remember a winter day so cold. I raced down to *Brigantia*'s cabin and picked up all three of my cardigans. I offered one to Habren. She smiled but looked puzzled. I had to show her how to put it on. Brigid declined hers, so I used it over the first as a shawl. 'Aren't you cold?' I asked, watching the clouds grow thicker and greyer and more and more heavy. Brigid shook her head. I realised that it was the presence of the sunlight that gave her her energy, and not the heat it radiated. She stood as she always stood, tall and delicately beautiful, yet stronger by far than me.

The leaves stopped their rustling. The birds were far too

frozen to sing. I pulled my woollens even tighter round me. My face was blue and I couldn't help but shiver. Habren stood stoically, as if used to loitering in sandals in the cold. Her nose was pinched, her face was still pale, but she was obviously determined not to complain.

Nodens and Brigid exchanged glances and Nodens grinned and nodded.

'What's going on?' I asked. Habren smiled knowingly but she said nothing.

'Wait and see,' Brigid said, touching her nose.

'Well, hurry up or I'll freeze to death,' I mumbled, and as I spoke I realised that the temperature was very slowly starting to rise. I looked at Nodens and Brigid and Habren, but they were totally absorbed, they stood side by side gazing fixedly up at the sky.

Suddenly snow began to fall. Huge great flakes drifted down like tiny parachutes with fluffy edges and crystal hearts. 'River flowers!' I exclaimed, clapping my hands in delight, and I forgot about feeling cold. I watched in amazement as the enormous, beautifully shaped flakes drifted down and settled over the water, delicately blanking every single bit of surface. Only when Lydney Sands was completely covered did I find my tongue . . . 'Why?'

'Coventina must see neither sun nor moon until she rises,' Nodens said.

'Why?'

'Brigid told you!' Habren said. 'The gates to the Other-world will only open in darkness, the rising has to be slow and gentle. Remember how Brigid struggled in panic and grabbed your legs as she rose? The light was too bright. It blinded her. It's too much of a shock until the eyes are properly focused. It's confusing.'

'You mean *I* rescued *her*!'

'Of course,' Nodens said, grinning as Brigid kicked his shins.

'If I'd have known that, I'd never have come.'

'We know, and that's why you didn't.'

'So was my falling an accident? Did I really slip?'

'You know you didn't,' Brigid giggled. 'You know you were born to the water.'

'So who pushed me?' I persisted.

Nodens hugged Brigid and winked at Habren and me. 'Time, the needs of time pushed you. Soon the new millennium will be born, soon the sunwheel begins a new circle.'

I gave up, it was all too confusing and, anyway, Brigid nudged me and pointed. I watched in silence as a white waterlily broke through the water and opened, rising higher and higher until I could see it was clutched by a woman's hand.

As Coventina rose the clouds gently lifted, the snow melted away as quietly as it had fallen, the sun broke through its blanket of grey and began to shine.

Coventina stood on a huge waterlily leaf. Gently, she floated towards me. In her left hand she clutched a large silver chalice that shone brightly in the light of the midday sun. 'Drink,' she commanded, holding the lip of the cup towards me.

'What is it?' I asked as she forced the liquid between my teeth.

'You must drink from the cauldron of Dagda. It will settle you into your new life.'

'What new life?'

Coventina was clearly irritated at being interrupted. She turned to Brigid. 'Daughter, are you sure?'

Brigid nodded. 'I'm sure. Ignore her, she hasn't changed much, she always answers back.'

'From this cup taste the liquor of the cauldron of Ceridwen, and receive all the knowledge you need.'

I sipped. I guessed it would be more hassle to refuse. Coventina offered her silver chalice a third and last time. 'Taste the kiss of Bran the blessed, for your rebirth is soon.'

'I'm not going anywhere except home,' I said but, to please them, I drank from the cup.

'You have drunk the very nectar of life,' Coventina said happily. 'I am free.'

'Coventina, my love!' Nodens said, feeling he could at last pull her close to him. 'I'm so sorry I lost my temper. It wasn't your fault Habren died, it was mine.'

'It was my *destiny* to die,' Habren said quietly.

'I wanted to say it's nobody's destiny to be murdered, but then I remembered Guendoloen had decreed that Habren was offered to Nodens, and Guendoloen was me. I stared uneasily at my toes, waiting for Habren to say more, but she just stood accepting her present as she had accepted her past.

'Doesn't anyone mind dying?' I asked.

Brigid shook her head. 'Dying is just a journey. You go to the Otherworld, you come back. What is there to fear?'

I didn't know so I shut up. Nodens and Coventina were mooning about like besotted young lovers.

'You can see why he has to hand over the rivers to Brigantia,' Brigid giggled. I nodded, smirking back, and even the quiet Habren smiled.

Coventina heard, she turned to her daughter. 'Brigid, darling, you know time is short and you have to move on.'

Brigid nodded, accepting like Habren, but I knew the questions in her head.

'Coventina, did you love her?' I asked. 'Did you love her even though she was never born?'

Coventina looked startled, as if the question was not needed. Brigid was *acting* all unconcerned. Coventina looked at me, then at Habren. Finally she reached out and clasped her daughter's hand.

'I love you, Brigid. I have loved you from the first

knowing. I will always love you. You may be unborn but you are still mine.'

Brigid raised her head and her eyes shone like stars. 'I love you. I loved the memories I was given, and I love the you who is.'

'Well that's everybody happy!' I said, winking at Habren.

While all this was going on, the skies darkened again. Habren was the first to notice. She eyed the sky then the land uneasily. Thunderbolts flashed across the sky, huge jagged streaks, great shiny sheets. Habren and Brigid looked frightened. Unease had turned to horror.

Water was everywhere, falling from the sky, rising from the land, higher and higher, even gushing from long-hidden springs in huge frothy flumes. It gushed across the sun-baked earth giving life to the dying rivers. Quiet waters became raging torrents, which tumbled and roared with the sheer exuberance of being.

Nodens and Coventina stood with love-struck eyes, each seeing only the other, not even feeling the rain. Brigid pushed them apart as she shouted, 'I told you to be vigilant! This is your last chance, Father. Look! It's Taran! Nodens, you have to go back. It's Taran and he's power crazy and about to take over!'

# 21 The sunwheel spins once more

Brigid, Habren and I watched in amazement as the water scrambled frantically over long-dry riverbed stones, rising rapidly up banks that had forgotten they were designed to constrain. The water began to rush down the hot dusty tracks, and all the time lightning flashed and thunder roared.

'So much, so fast!' Habren said, grabbing Brigid and shaking her. 'Brigid, I don't want to die, not again, not so soon!'

'It's too much, everyone will be killed!' I screeched at Brigid. 'People are falling into the waters and soon they will drown. I don't know what Nodens and Taran are doing but you have to stop it. Brigid, *do something*.'

'Enough will survive,' Brigid said quietly. 'Nodens and Taran are battling for control of the thunderclouds. Nodens has learned his lesson, this time he'll give of his best. The battle will soon be over. Nodens will not fail us again.'

'Soon is not enough!' I yelled. 'People are dying *now*.'

'Enough will survive to make life good. Those that die will not give their lives in vain. It is their sacrifice that gives us hope for the new millennium. We have come full circle. Soon the sunwheel will properly spin.'

I just gaped at Brigid.

'This is mass murder!' Habren shouted. 'It can't happen again. It musn't!'

'The people must learn the hard way how to subject themselves to the needs of Mother Earth who provides for them,' Brigid said sadly. 'How else can they build a future? They cannot always take, they must learn also to give. The land cannot properly contain so many people. A few must die for the good of all.'

'My mum and dad!' I yelled at Brigid. 'My mum and dad could be drowning. Have you no conscience? Brigid, do something, *please*!'

'This isn't up to me,' she said quietly. 'I can do nothing and neither can either of you. This battle is between Nodens and Taran.'

I looked up into the thick black sky, high above the sounds of choking children, high above the sounds of screaming women and the desperate struggle of drowning men.

Again and again the sky flashed brilliant orange. We screwed up our eyes to try and block out the brightness. The thunder was so loud our eardrums vibrated painfully, and all the time people were screaming or sinking into the waters of oblivion.

'Stop it! Mum and Dad mustn't die, not yet!'

'You said your mum lived at the top of a hill.'

'My dad . . .'

'Your dad won't go down to the pub in this, and your grandad can't.'

I shut up. I felt a little better, but not much. People were still dying while Brigid, Habren and I floated among the bloating bodies, safe in *Brigantia* and doing absolutely nothing to help. I threw over my lifebelts but, despite my frantic shouts, nobody saw.

'Taran's trying to take control of the new millennium,' Brigid explained as we moved *Brigantia* over what used to be land, towards higher ground. 'It's the war of all wars up there. Nodens is doing his best to stop him. Coventina has taken up her shield and gone to help. This time Coventina and Nodens will fight to the death for peace.'

I didn't know what to say, not with dead and dying bodies floating everywhere and people swimming so desperately for their lives. I could see husbands holding up wives and crying, women calling out for their missing children. 'Swim this way!' I yelled, but still nobody seemed aware of *Brigantia*, nobody came.

'Can't we help?' I pleaded. 'Can't we do anything?'

Brigid and Habren looked calm but sad. 'No,' they said together.

'I thought Brigantia was the clever one,' I stormed. 'I thought she was the efficient one. How come she's not where she should be?'

'She is!' Brigid said crossly. 'I've worked night and day to make it so.'

As we spoke the thunder gave one last giant roll and ceased. The water levelled but couldn't find space to recede more than slowly. The sky was still but uneasy, as if some dreadful truce was for the moment holding. The frantic people stared up at the sky, the fear of Taran making them silent.

'I have to go now,' I said, 'while it's calmer. Mum and Dad will be looking for me. Do you want to come with me, or wait for Nodens and Coventina?'

'You can't go,' Habren said.

'You have to stay,' Brigid agreed.

'I'm taking the boat and I'm going back.'

'You cannot go,' Habren and Brigid said together. 'Not

even if you want to. You have drunk from the cup of life.'

'So what?' I said, imagining Mum and Dad frantically searching the cut.

'So wait until the dawn of the millennium, just a few moments more. The water will have fallen back by then, you will be able to travel faster.'

I shrugged uneasily.

'Trust us,' Brigid said. 'Trust us and all will be well.'

I still didn't know. I still wasn't sure. We had grown so close, travelled so far. I felt as if they belonged to me, even the quiet placid Habren, who somehow instilled peace of mind by just standing close. I wanted to stay. I desperately wanted to stay, but I felt homesick. I wanted to know my mum and my dad were safe, even the grandad I barely remembered. I felt as if I was being split in two, divided.

'You are us,' Brigid said quietly. 'You cannot go.'

'We need you,' added Habren. 'Please stay a while more.'

Brigid removed the sunwheel from her neck and placed it round mine. To my surprise its presence felt comforting.

Out of the blackness of the strangely sullen sky rose the sun's first dawn ray. It struck the sunwheel, sending it spinning against my skin but it didn't burn or graze. In that moment I understood at last why choice was not mine. I took their hands and let Guendoloen rise for ever.

We held hands as the dawn cracked open the door of the new millennium. With the rising sun came not just the celebration fireworks, excited shouts and hooting horns that I had expected, but the absolute knowledge that this was the moment I was born. *This* was my birth day.

'I am Brigantia!' I announced. 'We are Brigantia.'

'I am the voice of the past, the face of the dead,' Habren said softly.

'I am the voice of the future, the hopes of the unborn,' Brigid whispered.

I needed no explanation. Like the rising sun I was growing stronger every moment.

'I am the present,' I affirmed softly. 'I am the experience called now. I am the link that makes us whole.'

'We are three and yet one. We are Brigantia, triple goddess of the rivers of life that the sunwheel turns. Because of us, you are you.'

# 22 Goodbye to *Brigantia*

When the waters had ebbed back to almost normal, Dad found *Brigantia*, leaking, empty, drifting.

'We should never have let her go!' Mum said, wringing her hands in despair when he told her. Dad said nothing. He took Mum's hand and I knew they were riddled with guilt. Grandad was feeling better than he'd been for years, Mum was happy in her garden, Dad had a little job, one he liked, but they'd left me, and look what had happened!

I couldn't stand their pain. I couldn't bear to leave them like that. I needed to tell them that death is nothing, just a rest in the Otherworld, but they couldn't hear, they wouldn't understand. I felt heartbroken, helpless. Then I remembered Den.

I *am* Brigantia, so Habren fetched Den back from the Otherworld and set him upon the gunwale. Brigid promised my land family healing and wished their futures well. I was left to walk the gunwales of *Brigantia* for the final time, with Den snuffling eagerly at my heels as he always did. My land family spotted him and smiled through their tears.

'Den's survived! I searched that boat and *he wasn't there before!*' Dad clutched Mum's hand tightly. 'There's another odd thing I should have told you – that painting, the one that was never finished, the shelf I put over it is missing. There's a goddess painted in the empty space, a triple goddess with three faces blended as one.' I held my breath, I knew what Dad was thinking, but he never said that one of the faces was mine.

'Gwen must have done it for us. Are you *sure* she drowned? Oh how I miss her, Corrie.'

'She's gone,' Dad said firmly, 'but in our hearts she'll live for ever.'

My heart ached with the need to tell them I loved them. They *were* my parents. I commanded Den to run round excitedly in circles as if I had only just arrived.

'Gwen *must* be there,' Mum whispered to Dad. 'See how Den wags his tail. He only ever goes that mad when she calls his name.'

Dad smiled through his tears. 'We're so lucky. She's come back to say goodbye.' Mum nodded. She smiled at Dad, the first small smile of healing.

Satisfied all would be well, I patted Den's head and sent him back to them, just a normal collie dog with a very waggy tail.

It was over, the end and the beginning. Her task complete, the boat *Brigantia* slipped quietly beneath the waters to rest in the Otherworld, and with her went Gwen, a boatie of no importance.

I lifted my arms triumphantly and raised my face to the shining sun.

*I am Brigantia. Nurture me and life will be well; neglect me and it will be at your peril.*

# Map of route

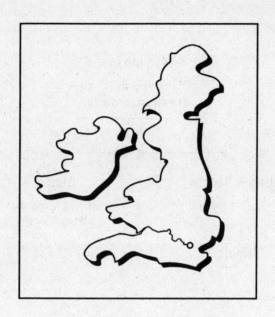

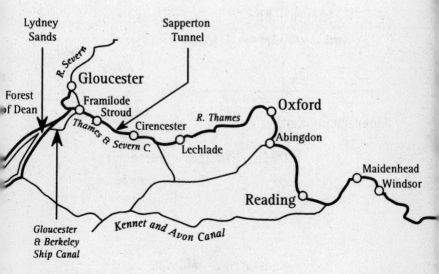

# Family trees

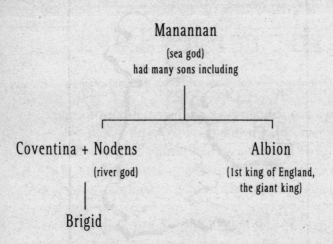

**Manannan**
(sea god)
had many sons including

**Coventina + Nodens**
(river god)

**Albion**
(1st king of England,
the giant king)

**Brigid**

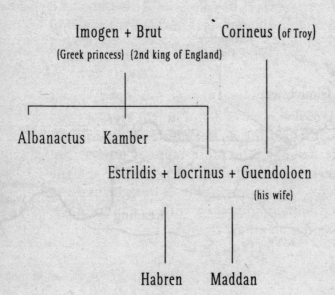

**Imogen + Brut**
(Greek princess)  (2nd king of England)

**Corineus** (of Troy)

**Albanactus  Kamber**

**Estrildis + Locrinus + Guendoloen**
(his wife)

**Habren  Maddan**

ELIZABETH ARNOLD

# The Parsley Parcel

Freya is a Romany – a chime child born to make the *most* difficult magic.

Freya must leave her family and her life of freedom to fulfil a promise and grant a wish. But, at the 'posh-polish' house of Emma and Jack Hemmingway, she feels stifled until she rescues Maggie, a magpie fledgling, and introduces some of the impulsive energy of her old life to the clean safe order of 'Aunt' Emma's world.

There is a clash of wills, tussles, laughter and tears and, in the end, love. But is love powerful enough to grant Emma's wish and set Freya free . . . ?

'a light-hearted and exuberant first novel . . . This story provides a wonderful insight into Romany life, of which the author creates a sympathetic understanding. The prose captures the scent of honeysuckle, the feel of open country and the freedom of a wandering life. It has a lightness of touch which, combined with gentle humour, makes this an enjoyable read.'
                                Junior Education

**ELIZABETH ARNOLD**

# Gold and Silver Water

*'I don't want to cross the line!'*
 *'Oh come on, Penny. It won't take a moment.'*
 *'But, Mum! The lights are flashing red!'*

A terrible accident and Penny, though physically unharmed, cannot talk, cannot even feel . . . She is lost in sadness.

Only one person can help – Freya, the chime child, with her Romany magic. Freya is given a clue by her crotchety great-gran. But can she discover the healing power of gold and silver water in time?

'An original book that gives you a real insight into Romanies and their fascinating traditions.'
*Daily Telegraph*